Once Bitten, Twice Shy

by

C.C. Wood

Table of Contents

Prologue

THE NIGHT WAS hot and moonless. The air I struggled to suck into my lungs felt wet and heavy. Even as I gasped in huge gulps, my lungs burned. My feet were bare. Rocks and twigs cut into the flesh of my feet, but I didn't stop. I couldn't. If I stopped running, he'd be on me.

I knew if he caught me that I was as good as dead. I also knew that he would take his time before I died. I would rather fight to the death than let him do those things to me. He had barely begun to hurt me when I escaped, but I knew without a doubt that I wouldn't let him get his hands on me again.

The punctures on my neck and arms were bleeding steadily. I felt my body weakening from the blood loss. My feet felt heavier with each step and the agonizing pain shot up from all the cuts and scrapes on the bottom of them. I didn't know how much longer I could go on, but I wasn't going to give up.

Suddenly, I burst out of the woods, into an open area. Before me I saw the spread of the lake and realized that he had herded me to a cliff. I came to a stop just a few feet from the edge, breathing heavily and almost collapsed to my knees. I was cornered.

I heard him approach and turned around. He wasn't loud, but I could make out the slight sound of his footsteps, the light, quick intake of his breath. He wasn't as winded as I. Actually, he wasn't winded at all. For some reason, that small detail enraged me. Probably because I was terrified and running for my life, and he was treating this as a game.

I watched as the hulking shadow emerged from the line of trees and my blood ran colder.

"Come to me," he whispered.

I felt my body respond. My feet took a step forward without my permission and I realized that the smirking bastard intended to make me walk to him so he could kill me. Somehow, I found the strength to resist and I stopped moving. I had nowhere to run, but at least I wasn't walking straight into the arms of death any longer.

"Come," he said.

I shook my head, fighting with every molecule in my body not to do as he said.

"Come," he roared.

Without my permission, my right foot lifted to take another step toward the shadow calling me.

I tried to stop. I tried to control the motions of my body, but there was nothing I could do. I bit my lip hard enough to break the skin and I tasted the sharp tang of blood. The pain broke his hold over me.

I screamed and turned so that I was facing the cliff. I fought his hold on my mind as I headed for the edge.

"COME TO ME!" His voice boomed, so loud my ears hurt.

Still, somehow, I fought his hold and took one more running step before I vaulted over the edge. I heard his scream of rage echo around me as I plummeted from the cliff. The rocks along the edge of the lake rushed up to meet me and there was a burst of bright light behind my eyes. Then I slid into blissful blackness.

Chapter One

I BURST OUT of the chains of the dream with a soundless scream. My throat was tight and my breathing so shallow that I didn't even have enough air to let loose the shriek that was caught in my chest. As they had in the dream, my lungs burned and the air I breathed didn't seem as though it was enough.

I realized that in my blind panic I had lunged out of bed and was standing next to the mattress, swaying. My legs collapsed beneath me and I fell to the floor, trying to slow my breathing. At first I didn't know where in the hell I was, but, as reality returned, I recognized my luxuriously appointed guest room. I was at the home my friend, Donna, shared with her fiancé, Conner. I was staying here with them while I recovered from the vampire attack I had suffered a few months ago.

Physically, I was fine, but my emotional state was still fragile. As much as I hated to admit it, I was a basket case. Because I couldn't handle my full-time workload any longer, I began to work from home just a few hours a week. Now, I could no longer afford my apartment, but the idea of going back out into the world on a regular basis gave me panic attacks. Though staying with vampires should have done the same, Donna was my best friend and, other than the whole drinking blood thing, she was no different now that she was a vampire. That alone made me feel safe in her house.

Finally, after several long minutes, my heart rate slowed and I actually felt as though I were sucking air into my lungs rather than glass. The adrenaline surge from the nightmare left me feeling weak, shaky, and nauseated. When I was somewhat certain that my legs would hold my weight, I pushed to my feet, leaning heavily against the bed until my knees didn't feel like cooked spaghetti.

I staggered to the sink in the bathroom and turned the cold water on full blast. Cupping the water in my hands, I splashed my sweaty, tear-streaked face and neck. The nausea threatened to overwhelm me, but I fought it back with everything I had. When I was certain I wouldn't be sick, I turned off the water and dried my face with a hand towel.

I realized that my sleep shirt was soaked with sweat and decided that a shower might help chase away the last dregs of the nightmare. I went to the shower and turned the water on. Now that I was up, my skin felt cold and clammy, so I turned the water to hot, stripped off my shirt and panties, and stepped under the steamy spray.

I showered quickly. My stomach was still upset and my hands were shaking as I washed my hair. A few minutes later, I finished rinsing the last of the sweat from my skin and stepped out of the shower. After I dried off, I realized that there was no way I would be able to go back to sleep.

I dressed in yoga pants and a t-shirt, leaving my feet bare. I knew Conner had tea in the well-stocked kitchen, so I padded out of the guest room and headed toward the stairs. It was only two in the morning and I knew that Conner and Donna would be snuggled up in their bed, even if they weren't sleeping.

Though I assumed they would probably still hear me, I tried to tiptoe down the stairs. It seemed so odd that they could hear me moving around on carpet, with bare feet, while their room was on the other side of the house, but it was something I was adjusting to. My best friend was a vampire. A rueful smile crossed my lips. The very sentence sounded deranged, but it was true.

Just a few months ago, I thought vampires were the stuff of legend and fantasy. Hell, I didn't even read paranormal romance. I often lost patience with the author's attempts at world building.

I learned the truth when Donna and I were kidnapped a month and a half ago, and I was still struggling with that knowledge and my own personal experiences with the fanged. When we had been taken by Vanessa, or the *shebitch with cuntitis* as Donna liked to call her, I thought I was going to die. Vanessa had given me to a fellow vampire who had explained in great detail what he intended to do to me before he would end my suffering with death.

As I walked down the stairs, I shivered at the memories. My dream tonight had brought them close to the surface. I hated that, because Donna and Conner would know and they would look at each other in that way that made me think they were having a conversation without speaking. Then Conner would avoid me the rest of the day and Donna would coddle me and drive me crazy.

Right after the attack, I hadn't wanted to see either of them again. I was convinced that all vampires must be soulless, demonic creatures with only the desire for blood and pain. All it had taken to change my mind was seeing Donna. I hadn't realized at the time that Conner had turned her. It wasn't until her eyes changed that I understood what happened.

At first, the fear was so overwhelming that I only wanted to run, to escape, but it became very clear within minutes that my friend was the same except in what she now needed for nourishment. Her personality, penchant for dropping the f-bomb, and her loyalty were all there.

Since I met Conner before knowing what he truly was, it was easier for me to accept him. It was the rest of vampire kind that I was having difficulty with. Each time I met a new vampire, it took all I had not to run away. The urge wasn't as strong now as it had been a couple of months ago, but it was still there. The few other vampires I'd met were friends of Conner's and they all treated me with care. Oddly, I found that their delicate treatment made me more comfortable.

Except for one, Alexander Dimitriades. He had a way of watching me that made me feel as though he were privy to my deepest thoughts and desires. And not because he was reading my mind, but because he was just that observant. His dark brown eyes were almost black and, whenever we were in the same room, I felt their weight against my skin like a physical caress.

I stepped wrong as I went down the stairs and had to grab the railing. Damn, I had to stop thinking about Alexander Dimitriades and focus on walking or I would end up with a broken neck. I forced myself to concentrate solely on navigating the steps in the dark hallway and nothing else.

I reached the bottom of the stairs safely and made my way to the kitchen. After my shower, my skin no longer felt ice cold, so I decided against hot tea and settled on sparkling water instead. I poured a glass over ice and headed out of the kitchen, passing through the room that housed the indoor pool on my way to the veranda.

It was a hot night, so I stepped out and shut the sliding door behind me. I sipped my water and sighed as a slight breeze caressed my face and lifted my hair away from my neck. Though my skin was no longer cold, my insides felt frozen. As the warm breeze flowed around me, I felt myself thaw.

The veranda ran the entire length of the rear of the house, which meant it was huge. There were seating areas, gliders, and even a porch swing, every few feet. I headed to the porch swing and sat on the padded surface, tucking one of my legs beneath me.

I turned my face toward the breeze and lifted my head. I sighed again as the scent of Carolina Jessamine and honeysuckle curled around me, light and sweet. Sitting outside in the dark, warm night, I felt a sense of peace spreading within me. I drank the rest of my water and placed the glass on the small table next to the swing. I used the toe of my other foot to push off and set the swing in motion.

Just as I was beginning to truly relax, a shadow detached from the darkness and moved toward me. I stiffened and opened my mouth to scream when the dark shape spoke.

"It is only me."

As though I had conjured him with my earlier thoughts, Alexander Dimitriades stood before me, wearing nothing but a pair of black lounge pants and shadows. His olive skin stretched taut over bulky but defined muscles. I struggled not to stare as my mouth went dry. Too bad I had already drunk the rest of my water because I suddenly needed it badly. I had no idea what he was doing here. I knew he met with Conner earlier in the study, but I assumed he left afterwards.

My back remained stiff as he moved toward me, his feet silent as he crossed the veranda. I had the vague sense that I was being stalked by a predator and felt a chill race down my spine. Goosebumps broke out on my arms even though the night had to be close to 80 degrees Fahrenheit.

As I watched him, I realized why. He moved like a large cat, graceful but with coiled strength, just waiting for the opportunity to pounce. I couldn't say why, but that thought both terrified and excited me.

I didn't speak as he came closer and used his hip to shove me to the side so he could sit with me. Because he was so tall and broad, there was very little room on the swing for both of us. In fact, my entire side was touching his and I was all but crammed against the arm of the seat.

As though he sensed this, Alexander raised the arm closest to me and laid it along the back of the swing. His fingertips grazed the bare skin of my shoulder where the large neck of my t-shirt had shifted. I shivered as another chill moved down my vertebrae. This time for very different reasons.

I cleared my throat, which felt inexplicably tight. "You decided to stay the night?" I asked lightly, desperately trying to be casual, even though my heart was beginning to pound against my sternum.

"Yes, Conner asked me to," he replied.

As it wasn't my house, I didn't probe that subject any further. Conner could ask whoever he wanted to stay the night.

I changed the subject. "Couldn't sleep?"

"No. You?"

"Not really," I replied.

"Why?" His voice was quiet but I could still hear a trace of his Greek accent.

I shrugged. "It's not home, I suppose." There was no way I was explaining my nightmares to him.

He nodded and looked out on the backyard. His thumb moved lightly against the skin of my shoulder. I tried to shift away, but only managed to dislodge the neck of my t-shirt further, leaving more skin exposed. Alexander continued to trace random patterns against my flesh.

My only alternatives were to lean away from his hand, which would plaster me against his side, or to get off that damn swing pronto. I chose the latter.

I started to rise, but his hand landed on my shoulder, keeping me in my seat. My heart rate went from somewhat normal, to a fast and frantic pace. Oh, God.

"Calm, Ivie. I'm not going to hurt you." He sighed. "I find it pleasant to sit with you."

I swallowed my panic. "Look, Alexander," I started.

He interrupted me. "Call me Lex."

Okay, fine, whatever it took to get off this damn swing and back to the dubious safety of my room.

"Look, Lex, I'm tired, I think I'm going to head back to bed."

This time he didn't stop me when I scrambled to my feet. Instead, he stood with me, but he was too close. My chest tightened and I stumbled. Lex's hands closed lightly around my elbows, keeping me upright.

"Careful," he said softly.

I could feel the flutter of my pulse in my throat as I stared up at him. I wasn't a tall woman, topping out at five-foot four, and Lex towered over me. He had to be six-two or six-three, easily. The shadows under the veranda hid most of his features from me but his eyes gleamed. I realized then that my hands were curved around his biceps. His rock hard biceps. Surprisingly, his skin was warm, almost hot.

Unable to tear my eyes away, I stared at the muscles in his arms, following the dips and bulges of his shoulders to his chest. I realized I was practically drooling on him and my eyes shot to his face. I saw a flash of white teeth and almost flinched before I realized he was smirking at me rather than coming in for the kill.

One of his hands lifted to my hair, wrapping a hank of it around his index finger. "Why are you afraid of me, little one? Do you think I would hurt you?"

Somehow the truth spilled out of my mouth without my permission. "I don't know. I've been hurt before by your kind."

The movement of his hand in my hair stilled and I felt the muscles of his arms harden further under my hands. This time I did flinch, worried that he was angry with me for my blunt words. His hand shifted from my hair to my cheek, but his touch was incredibly gentle.

"Never by me. Please do not blame the rest of my people for the brutality of a few. Just as there is evil among humans, there is also evil among vampires."

I couldn't argue with that because it was the truth. Still, he made me extremely nervous. I swallowed hard and wet my lips.

"Okay." My voice lacked conviction.

The corner of his mouth lifted up. "You'll see."

I nodded, just wanting to get the hell out of there, but Lex continued to stare at me. Considering how dark it was, I couldn't see his expression, but I was sure he could see my face clearly. Donna told me vampires had phenomenal vision, even if it was almost pitch black.

I wasn't sure what he saw as he looked at me, but he took a step back and removed his hand from my face.

"Goodnight, little one," he said.

"Night," I mumbled before I skirted around him and practically ran into the house.

I felt his eyes on me until I disappeared through the door.

Chapter Two

THE NEXT MORNING, I dragged myself out of bed. I felt like someone had beaten me during the night because I hadn't gone back to sleep after my late night run-in with Lex. I was exhausted. Still bleary-eyed, I staggered down the stairs and into the kitchen.

Donna stood by the coffee maker with a steaming mug of coffee in her hand and another on the counter next to her. When she saw me, she nodded to the cup.

"That one's yours," she said.

"You are a goddess," I mumbled.

I snatched up the cup and sucked in a huge sip. The coffee was hot and strong. In other words, perfect. Donna smirked at me, but I could see the concern on her face.

"Rough night?" she asked.

I sipped my coffee and shrugged one shoulder. I honestly didn't want to talk about it.

It became clear to me that Donna wasn't going to let it go when she said, "I heard you get up. Was it the same nightmare again? The one where you're being chased through the woods?"

I scowled at my coffee and drank more. She was still standing there, looking at me, waiting, when I lowered the mug.

I sighed. "Do you have to ruin such a good cup of coffee with this conversation?"

"Yes," she answered.

"Fine," I huffed. "Yes, I had that nightmare again. And, no, I couldn't go back to sleep. I got up and drank some water and had the shit scared out of me by your hubby's skulking friend."

Donna's brows lowered. "He's not my hubby yet. And I don't think it would be smart to talk about Lex while he's in the house. That man has sonic hearing, even better than a typical vampire's."

I shivered when she said the V-word. Then I did it again when I realized that Lex probably heard everything I just said, no matter what part of the house he was in. "Really?" I squeaked.

"Seriously," she said, nodding her head. "Plus, that man is scary intense when it comes to you."

I took a huge gulp of my coffee, coughing a little when the hot liquid poured down my throat.

"Are you sure you don't want Conner to wipe your memory of the event, Ivie? He said he could do it. That you would remember you had been taken, but not the actual details."

This wasn't the first time that she offered, but it was the first time I was tempted. The nightmares were still plaguing me months later. I wasn't sleeping, I was barely eating. For the first time in my life, I was losing weight without really trying. My mother, who was constantly on my ass about my weight, would be so proud. It seemed that getting kidnapped and attacked by a vampire was the best diet available.

I hadn't told Donna the whole story of my abduction. I don't know why, but I just couldn't share the details with her. The fear, the pain, the things that *monster* said he wanted to do to me. Just the memory made my skin break out in a cold sweat.

I opened my mouth to tell her yes, that I did want Conner to wipe my memory, but I couldn't do it. It felt weak and I was not weak. There were people in the world that had been attacked and suffered much worse than I had. They didn't have the option to forget and they recovered. I could do the same.

I closed my mouth and shook my head. "No, I can deal. It's just going to take a little time."

Donna's expression said loud and clear that she didn't believe me, but I ignored her and continued to drink my coffee.

"Well, if you change your mind…" she trailed off as I just looked at her over my coffee cup and raised a brow. "Don't lift your damn eyebrow at me! I just want to help." She paused. "And how the hell do you lift just one eyebrow anyway? I can never do that."

I smirked at her but didn't answer.

"Good morning."

At the sound of that Scottish brogue, Donna and I both turned to the door to watch her fiancé, Conner, saunter into the kitchen. It was barely seven in the morning and he was already showered and dressed in a gray suit that was perfectly tailored. I knew it had to cost more than one month's rent on my apartment because the fabric had a subtle sheen I'd only seen on the most expensive designer suits. His shirt was a lighter gray and his tie was almost white the gray was so pale. It was a good look.

Conner grinned at me and I realized he knew I was drooling over him.

I glanced over my shoulder at Donna, knowing that she would be able to hear my thoughts if I was broadcasting them that loudly. "Sorry."

It was her turn to smirk. "It's okay. Fangboy is a hottie."

I couldn't help it. I snorted as I laughed. I didn't know if I would ever get used to the fact that one of my best friends could now snatch thoughts out of my head, hypnotize me into doing whatever she wanted, and drink blood. It was mind-boggling. Though the hypnotizing thing might come in handy if one of my co-workers ever pissed me off. I was pretty sure Donna would be more than happy to make my boss think he was a spider monkey and brainwash him so that he would go around humping office furniture while howling at the top of his lungs.

When she giggled, I knew that she read my mind again.

"Stop that!" I snapped.

"Well stop blaring your thoughts at top volume and I'll stay out of them!" Donna argued.

I sighed and rolled my eyes, lifting my cup to drain the last of my coffee. After months, I should have been much better at controlling my thoughts.

Conner was still grinning at our byplay, and likely the wild images I was thinking, as he sauntered over to the coffeemaker. After he poured himself a mug, he brought the carafe to me and poured more coffee into my mug.

"Thanks," I said.

He was still smiling, his gorgeous blue eyes twinkling with humor. "You're welcome."

I grabbed the sugar bowl and creamer and doctored my coffee so that it was sweet and light, the way I liked it. As I stirred the hot liquid, I felt him enter the room. I don't know why, but it seemed like every nerve ending in my body snapped to attention whenever he got within a hundred feet of me.

"Good morning."

I shivered at the sound of Lex's sexy, deep voice. His accent was barely noticeable, but still enough to make every word he spoke sound incredible. He probably could have read the ingredient list off a cereal box and I would find it hot as hell.

"Morning," I mumbled into my cup.

Donna gave me a wide-eyed look before she spoke, "Good morning, Lex. Did you sleep well?"

I smelled the light, clean scent of his skin as he walked by me and it was all I could do not to start sniffing his shoulder. I wasn't sure if it was merely soap or if he wore cologne, but he smelled fantastic all the time.

"I had a pleasant night," he answered cryptically.

I felt heat rise up into my cheeks at his reference to our late night encounter. I avoided Donna's eyes by watching Lex open a cabinet to remove a cup and fill it with hot coffee. Somehow I became absorbed in watching his large hands cradle the mug. Before I could start imagining those hands cupping parts of my body, I shook myself out of the trance. There was no need to share my sexual fantasies with the vampires.

"Okay, I'm going to run upstairs and get dressed," I said before I left the room. I managed to walk sedately rather than dash back up the stairs, so that none of the nosy vampires would know that I was fleeing the kitchen like a whore at a Baptist tent revival.

I hid in my room, taking a shower even though I had showered the night before. I wanted to wait as long as possible before going downstairs. I put product in my curly, dark hair and even blow dried it so that it fell in intentional disarray. Then I applied my make-up and slipped into my favorite black pants and a black shirt. Almost all of my clothes were black for two reasons. One, it made it much simpler to get dressed in the morning and, two, black was slimming.

I glanced at the clock and realized that I had been upstairs for over an hour and, for the first time in a week, I was actually hungry. I slipped out of my room and headed downstairs to the kitchen. I met Donna in the front hall and jumped.

"Dammit. Wear a bell or something, Dee. You scared the shit out of me," I complained.

"I can't help it if you're clomping down the hall like a herd of elephants and you didn't hear me."

I rolled my eyes. "Whatever." My stomach growled.

Donna's eyes widened. "Hungry there, Sigourney Weaver?"

I scoffed at her Alien reference and continued toward the kitchen. "Sigourney Weaver's character was never infected in the first movie."

I ignored whatever her response was because when I entered the kitchen, I smelled something heavenly. I made a beeline for the pot on the stove. I heard Donna come in behind me and laugh.

"Lex put a stew together for our lunch this morning before the guys left," she said.

I jerked my hand back from the lid of the pot as though I'd burned myself. "What?"

She went to the fridge and pulled out a bottle of water before she went to the bar and sat down on a stool.

"Yeah. He knew you hadn't eaten breakfast and said you were losing too much weight. He put all that together in like fifteen minutes and told me to make sure you ate a bowl of it around noon."

I stared at her blankly for a few seconds. "He said I'm losing too much weight?" I asked incredulously.

I was short, but not a small woman. In fact, my mother, who had been the same size since high school, gave me a huge guilt trip about my weight almost every time we spoke. I even had a bit of a complex about it. I had curves and I likely always would. No way in hell would I starve myself to fit what society considered the 'norm'. Did I want to be healthier? Yes, but I didn't necessarily think those stick-thin women were healthy either. A person who enjoyed good nutrition shouldn't be able to count every rib.

Donna smirked at me. "Yeah, apparently the Greek god agrees with me that you're gorgeous just the way you are."

I realized I was gaping at her and snapped my mouth shut. I'd broken up with my boyfriend almost a year ago, but had avoided dating since because of that pesky little neurosis about my weight. The idea that a man as gorgeous as Alexander Dimitriades could find me attractive was almost unbelievable.

She just shook her head at me. "How you can't see how beautiful you are when you look in the mirror every morning, I will never understand."

I just gave her a dirty look and headed to the fridge. I found bagels and cream cheese and decided that sounded perfect. I ignored Donna as I prepared my breakfast. I wanted to refuse to eat the stew that Lex had made. I almost couldn't believe he could do something as domesticated as preparing a meal. Mostly because he looked like the Greek warrior he'd likely been, with bulky muscles and animalistic grace.

When I finished toasting my bagel and smearing it with cream cheese, I looked up to find Donna watching me closely.

"What?" I asked as I put the bagels and cream cheese back in the fridge. I spied a container of orange juice and pulled it out to pour myself a glass.

"How do you feel about Lex?" she asked almost hesitantly.

I turned to get a glass out of the cabinet, glad to have a chance to put my back to her. I was a little afraid of what she might read from my expression.

"He seems nice," I mumbled.

I kept my back to her as I carefully poured my juice and put the juice carton back in the fridge. I grabbed my breakfast and sat at the counter next to her.

Donna's hand moved to rest on my wrist. "Then why did you run out of here this morning like your ass was on fire?"

Shit, she'd noticed.

Donna continued. "Are you frightened of him?" She paused. "I can promise you that he will never hurt you. Lex may look big and scary, but he's really a teddy bear."

I didn't believe the last part of her statement for a second, but, strangely, I did think she was right that Lex would never hurt me. I just shrugged in response.

"Ivie, look at me."

I forced myself to meet her eyes though I really, *really* did not want to be having this conversation.

"Are you scared of Lex?" she asked earnestly.

I sighed. "No, Dee. I'm not afraid of him. I don't think he'll hurt me. After being around you and Conner and a few of your friends, I'm beginning to understand that there are good and bad vampires, just like there are different types of people in the world. Still, I am afraid of how he makes me feel."

She looked at me quizzically, waiting for me to explain.

"He makes me feel..." I stopped speaking, searching for the right word. "Twitchy," I finished lamely.

It wasn't exactly accurate, but it was the best I could do. I honestly didn't think I could explain the feelings that Lex evoked. I always felt as though my entire body was on red alert whenever he was around.

As she watched me, Donna began to smile. "You like him," she said.

I shook my head vehemently. "No, that's not what I mean."

She just kept speaking. "You do! He makes you nervous!"

I couldn't dispute that, so I just shrugged and took a bite of my bagel.

Donna grinned and clapped her hands in excitement. "Awesome! Maybe the four of us can go on a double date or something. I knew Lex had a bit of a thing for you, but I didn't realize that you returned the feelings. This is great! I'm so glad that you don't still think he's a monster."

I started shaking my head at her as she spoke. When she finished, I answered, "Not gonna happen, Dee. Just because I think he's pretty and he makes me twitchy doesn't mean that I want to date him. I think it's for the best if I just avoid him all together."

Her head cocked to the side and the smile disappeared from her face. "Why? Because he's a vampire?"

Again, I didn't have a real answer, so I shrugged.

"Don't shrug at me, Ivie Lang. Talk to me," she demanded.

I sipped my orange juice because my mouth was suddenly dry. I could tell that the idea that I wouldn't want Lex because he was a vampire bothered her. I could understand that. She was a vampire now and I knew she secretly worried that I would sever our friendship. In all honesty, that was my first instinct after I had learned what she was. Now that I'd had time to adjust, I wouldn't dream of it. But to have a romantic relationship with a vampire? No way. Where in the hell could that go? I mean, that was like me having a romantic relationship with a cow. You didn't have relationships with your food. Well, maybe you did if it was chocolate. God knew I had an extreme fondness for it. I was food as far as a vampire would be concerned. He might drink my blood. He might even want to fuck me, but he probably would never love me.

For once, I must have managed to hide my thoughts from Donna, because she didn't even blink as all these notions were whirling through my mind. I was glad. I didn't want to have this argument with her. I knew that she would start talking about being Claimed, but that ended one way. With her being changed into a vampire. It seemed to me that vamps couldn't love us puny humans unless we became like them.

Finally, I broke eye contact and took another sip of my orange juice. "Can we not talk about this anymore, Dee? It's ruining my appetite."

That wasn't a lie. All this conversation about Lex, God, *dating* Lex of all things, made the few bites of bagel I had eaten sit in my stomach like lead.

Donna stared at me for a few more moments, but relented. "Sure. We can talk about something else." She paused. "Hey! Let's go shopping this afternoon."

I blinked at her. Donna hated shopping. Conner had to drag her to the store if she ever needed clothes for particular events.

"You want to go shopping?" I asked, my voice two octaves higher than usual and completely disbelieving.

"I like to shop," she said defensively.

I shook my head and took a bite of my bagel, distracted from my funk by her completely out-of-character behavior. "No you don't. You said shopping is the only form of torture that would ever break you if you were captured by North Koreans."

She gave a disgusted sigh and slumped down. "Okay, you're right. I don't know why I said that. I just don't want you to sit around here and mope." Then she perked back up again. "How about a movie?"

That actually did sound fun. "Okay. What do we want to go see?"

"How about the new movie with Bradley Cooper in it?" she asked.

"Mmmmm...Bradley Cooper. That sounds great."

She grabbed her smart phone and started clicking away. "I'll check the show times. We can go after you eat a bowl of Lex's stew."

With that final comment, I gave up on my bagel and got up to toss it in the trash. Just the mention of his name made my stomach clench. The damn man was fucking with my head even though he was nowhere near me.

Chapter Three

THAT NIGHT, AFTER Donna and I spent the day hanging out and going to the movies, we were sitting in the hot tub, drinking wine. It had been a wonderful, relaxing day, one of the best I'd had since the attack. Wearing my utilitarian black swimsuit, I let my head loll back against the side of the hot tub and took a deep drink of the red wine Donna had opened. It was superb.

"This is better than sex," I murmured, my eyes closed.

Donna snorted. "No, it isn't."

I sighed. "Okay, so it's not better than good sex, but it is better than the sex I had before Stanley and I broke up."

"What did you expect? His name was Stanley, he was five-five, skinny, and wore a pocket protector."

I opened one eye to give her a harsh stare. "Don't judge a book by its cover, okay? He was very sweet and funny as hell. He was just too…" I paused, "tame in the bedroom."

Donna chuckled, knowing my interest in adventurous activities. "Surely he could have been taught."

I closed my eyes again. "Maybe, but he decided his promotion and the move to California was more important that his relationship with me, so it's moot at this point."

I felt rather than heard Donna sit up straighter in the water. "The boys are home."

I smirked. Boys, my ass. Conner and Lex were M-E-N. Only Donna could get away with calling her fiancé and his large, muscular friend boys.

A few minutes later, the soft click of dress shoes echoed in the huge room that housed the indoor pool and hot tub. I knew Conner and Lex were making an effort not to startle me with their approach. I appreciated it. I knew from experience that vampires could move soundlessly when they wanted to.

"Hey, Fangboy, how was your day?" Donna asked sweetly.

Conner sighed. "Lass, how many times must I ask you not to call me by that wretched nickname?"

Cheekily, Donna replied, "One more."

He chuckled as he approached the hot tub and I sat up straight and opened my eyes. I could feel Lex coming closer as well because I could swear the temperature of the water went up another twenty degrees. Or it could have just been the panty-melting kiss Conner laid on Donna.

"How was your day?" he asked as he pulled away from Donna. There were wet handprints all over the fancy material of his suit, but he didn't seem to mind.

I glanced over my shoulder at Lex and dipped my chin in a silent hello. He might make me uncomfortable, but my mother raised me to be polite. His chocolate brown eyes were warm and amused as he smirked at me. I barely refrained from rolling my eyes at him and turned back around, sipping my wine.

"Great. Ivie and I went to the movies and just spent the day hanging out." Her eyes shifted over my shoulder to Lex. "The stew was delicious, by the way."

Lex's voice sounded directly behind me and above my head when he answered. "Thank you."

I stiffened as I felt the tip of his finger trace lightly down the nape of my neck. I sat up and moved away from the edge, twisting to face him, glad to have an excuse to keep him from touching me.

"No, thank you, Lex. It was very good," I said.

He had a hand on the edge of the hot tub, the other tucked into his pocket. With his sharp suit, five o'clock shadow, and casual stance, he looked like he belonged on the cover of GQ or Vogue.

"You're welcome, little one," he answered.

I heard Donna's breath hitch slightly behind me and gritted my teeth. Now, she would never let up about that stupid double date idea.

Sure enough, I heard her set her wine glass down with a click. "Hey, why don't you guys grab some suits and jump in here with us?"

"That sounds wonderful, lass," Conner answered. He looked to Lex. "There are a couple pairs of extra trunks in the changing room."

They walked together to the spacious changing room in the back corner of the pool area. As soon as they shut the door behind them, I shifted across the hot tub and put my mouth directly next to Donna's ear.

"I know exactly what you're trying to do, Dee, and I really don't appreciate it," I hissed.

She gave me wide, innocent eyes and I growled low in my throat.

"Don't try to play me. Vamp or not, I read you like a book and I told you earlier that there will never be anything between Lex and

I." I said this almost soundlessly, hoping that Conner and Lex couldn't hear me over the noise of the hot tub.

She leaned closer. "I think he would be good for you. Why can't you just give him a chance?"

I shook my head. I couldn't tell her the real reason because, vampire or not, she was my friend first and I didn't want to hurt her feelings by explaining the whole food chain thing that bugged the shit out of me.

"I'm just not ready to date, Dee. He also doesn't strike me as the type to have serious relationships."

She scoffed. "You've said maybe fifty words to him since you met him. How would you know that?"

I clamped my mouth shut and glared at her. I heard the dressing room door open so I moved back to my side of the hot tub, my eyes telling Donna that I would get revenge for the awkward position she put me in and that she should watch her back. I realized then that she, Conner, and Lex could probably hear every word I was thinking about her, so I took a deep breath and forced myself to calm down.

By the time Lex and Conner reached the hot tub, I was no longer thinking about putting used chewing gum in the toes of Donna's Louboutins. Then, when I saw Lex standing next to the tub in nothing but a pair of brief, tight trunks, I wasn't angry at all. Rather than wearing the board shorts popular in America, he had chosen swimming trunks that were normally worn in Europe or the Bahamas. They looked like snug boxer briefs.

I managed to jerk my eyes away from his almost naked body, but the image was burned into my retinas. Broad shoulders, carved abs, and bulging thighs. Actually, his thighs weren't the only noticeable bulge, but I shoved that thought out of my head immediately. I didn't need to be thinking about what Lex was packing in his trunks. Especially when everyone in the room could read my mind if they wanted. Or hear my thoughts if I couldn't control how loudly I was broadcasting them.

Lex and Conner climbed into the tub with us. Conner immediately moved toward Donna, lifting her up and setting her in his lap. She laughed loudly as he stuck his face into her neck. Though the hot tub was large enough for ten people, Lex chose the seat on the bench next to me. In fact, he sat so closely that our legs touched from hip to knee. Then he leaned back against the side and rested an arm behind me, the bare skin of his torso pressing against my side.

I jumped at the contact, but his hand landed on my shoulder to keep me from moving away. He'd used the same move last night. I realized that it felt possessive, as though he was claiming me in front of Donna and Conner. It was also blatantly dominant and his way of telling me to sit and stay.

I wanted to hate it, but I felt a long dormant, secret part of me quiver in interest. A few years ago, I had become fascinated with the idea of being dominated. After a few unexciting attempts with my then boyfriend, I decided it wasn't for me. It didn't make my blood run hot the way the books I'd read had. I figured it was one of those things that sounded sexier on paper than in reality.

Now I was beginning to suspect that it was because my boyfriend wasn't really a Dom. Because, when Lex did things to control me, it made my blood heat and the place between my thighs tingle. I shifted slightly, putting a sliver of space between our bodies, but only because Lex allowed it.

There was a moment of awkward silence. I was grateful as Donna and Conner drew Lex and I into small talk. If nothing else, it helped distract me from the sensation of Lex's bare leg against mine and his hand burning a brand into the flesh of my shoulder.

"So, where did you go today?" Donna asked.

Conner glanced at me. "Lass, I don't know if we should have this discussion now."

Donna saw the glance and her eyebrows lowered. Squinty-eyed, she leaned closer to him. "Why not? Ivie would never rat us out."

Conner spoke to me directly. "I don't believe you would ever willingly tell anyone details that you heard, but, as a human, you are susceptible to mind control and almost any vampire would be able to force their way into your thoughts if they wished. It is safer for you, and for us, if you don't have details."

Donna's eyes widened. "Oh shit, I never thought of that. Will she be in danger just because she's staying with us?"

Conner shook his head and sighed. "No more than she was before, lass. Though I doubt she thinks that being kidnapped with you was safe."

He was right, I didn't find that comforting. I flinched inwardly at his words. That was exactly why I would not be getting involved with Lex. Though I knew he hadn't meant to hurt me, Conner's statement proved my intuition had been correct. I wasn't to be trusted because I was human.

I must not have hidden my wince well because both Conner and Lex turned to look at me quizzically. I merely gave them both a small smile.

To Donna, I said, "It's okay, Dee. I don't want to do anything that would put any of you in danger. It's probably best if I don't know."

She studied me intently for a few moments before she sighed. "Fine." Donna looked at Conner, "So what can you tell us?"

I completely missed Conner's reply because Lex's lips touched the shell of my ear.

"Why did you flinch, little one?" he whispered.

I shot him a sideways glare. "I have no idea what you mean," I lied.

I jumped as a sharp pain radiated from my ear. Holy shit, had he just bitten me? His lips closed around my earlobe and he sucked gently, removing the pain. I felt his mouth *everywhere*. I tried to lean away, but he wouldn't let me.

"Don't ever lie to me, Ivie. I will never invade your mind without your permission, but I will always know when you lie. I forbid it," he said in my ear. His voice was stern, almost cold.

Though I wanted to mindlessly agree because I hated the tone of his voice at that moment, I also couldn't control the defiance that filled me.

I turned and glared at him. "I don't believe you have the right to demand anything from me, or forbid me to do anything," I whispered harshly. I was very aware that, even though they were speaking, Donna and Conner were probably listening to every word of my exchange with Lex.

He leaned even closer, his dark eyes brightening with an eerie glow. "I have every right."

I had never liked being told what to do. However, I couldn't deny that Lex's bossiness was a bit of a turn on. Still, I couldn't let him have the upper hand. I couldn't stop the little growl that escaped my throat.

At the noise, his eyes returned to their usual deep brown and he blinked, his brows rising on his forehead. Apparently, my resistance surprised him.

"Did you just growl at me?" he asked incredulously.

I felt the heat crawling up my chest and neck to my cheeks and knew I was blushing from my cleavage to my hairline.

"Um," I paused, searching for some other way to describe the noise I made. There was none.

It was my turn to be shocked as Lex threw back his head and literally roared with laughter. I hadn't been around him much, but I knew that Alexander Dimitriades smiled very little and I'd never seen him laugh in the handful of times we had spoken. Or the greater number of times I had watched him from a distance as he interacted with others.

I realized that Conner and Donna were silent and looked at them. Conner was grinning at me, his bright blue eyes twinkling with mischief. Donna's mouth was hanging open as she stared at Lex. I realized that my assumption had been correct. Lex didn't laugh and, somehow, my behavior had amused him greatly. His laughter was echoing in the cavernous room, it was so loud.

"Lass, it's almost ten and I am tired. I think it is time for us to retire," Conner said.

I felt my eyes widen and I stared at Donna with desperation. She couldn't abandon me. She only gave me a lopsided grin and followed Conner out of the hot tub.

I watched them for a moment, frozen with anxiety. When I realized that my best friend was about to ditch me, I turned to Lex.

"I'm really exhausted, Lex. You know, with the insomnia and everything last night. I think I'm going to head to bed, too."

His expression was inscrutable, but he didn't respond so I slid off the bench in the hot tub and started to head toward the steps that led out of the water. Before I got more than a foot from him, his hand closed around my arm and he yanked me back against his chest.

When the bare skin of my back touched his naked torso, I thought I was going to faint. His skin was hot, hotter than the water, and I was sure that my own skin would melt until I fused to him. Though that seemed frighteningly appealing.

I shook off the strange thoughts and tried to remain calm. I looked up over my shoulder at him. All I could see was the tight line of his stubbled jaw.

"What are you doing?" I asked. I tried to keep my voice cold, aloof, but it came out more like a squeak.

"We need to finish our conversation, Ivie, then you may go to bed."

Every muscle in my body went rigid. "And I think I've made it perfectly clear that you can't tell me what to do."

His hands tightened slightly on my arms before they opened and slid down. He wrapped his arms around my waist and sat back on the bench, wedging my ass between his thighs. I felt something hard and large press against my upper ass and tried to pull away. Holy shit, he had an erection to rival Reunion Tower in downtown Dallas.

Lex held me still with very little effort. "Calm down."

"Let me go," I demanded between clenched teeth.

"No."

"I refuse to talk to you until you let me go," I said, my voice going up two octaves from the crazy seesaw of emotions going on inside of me.

"Ah, you can feel what you do to me, can't you?" Unbelievably, the arrogant vampire pressed his hips closer to mine.

If any other man were doing this to me, I would have been enraged, biting and clawing to break free. With Lex, I was irritated but I was also aroused. He didn't want to let me go, so he wasn't going to. He was strong enough to keep me exactly where he wanted me and there was nothing I could do about it. Apparently, I was kinkier than I thought because that flipped my switch, big time.

Finally, I let my body relax against him. I felt more than heard his sigh. Still, a part of me wasn't ready to give up yet. I had learned the hard way to be wary of vampires.

"Say what you have to say, Alexander. I am very tired." I was proud of my composure, though I hated that I sounded as though I had a huge stick up my ass.

"Why did you flinch, Ivie?"

Damn, I did not want to have this conversation. I bit my lip, but didn't respond. His hands moved up and down my biceps in a small caress.

"Tell me, little one," his deep, slightly accented voice was gentle, almost sweet. "What did Conner say that upset you? Are you worried that you are in danger?"

His concern worked far better than coercion to convince me to talk to him. I lowered my head and closed my eyes.

"I knew I would be in danger when I moved in here. Conner and Donna didn't want me to know, but I can still tell what Donna is thinking. And when she's scared." I sighed. "I hate that Conner doesn't feel as though I can be trusted. I would never do anything to hurt Donna."

Lex's hands tightened on my arms. Somehow, my words surprised him. I don't know how I knew that, but I just did.

"Conner knows you are trustworthy. Unfortunately, you do not have the same characteristics that Donna possessed before she was turned. She was immune to vampire mind tricks. They understand that you would never willingly tell anyone things about them. Still, you could be forced and it would be clear very quickly that we kept you out of our secrets. It is safer for you should you be caught."

I shrugged slightly. I understood, but I didn't like it. Lex pulled me a fraction of an inch closer before he loosened his grip on my arms.

"Try to get some rest, little one. You are losing weight and not sleeping. I want you to be healthy." He paused and tension built in my belly. "You'll need to be well for what I have planned for you."

I shivered and he released me. I surged through the water to the side of the hot tub and climbed out. I didn't even give a shit if it seemed like I was running away. Probably because I was. I just wanted out of there before I did something stupid like climb into his lap and beg him to do whatever he wanted to me.

I had never been so conflicted in my life. I wrapped up in my robe and walked quickly out of the room. With each step, I could feel the weight of Lex's dark brown eyes on my back. When I made it to the door, I waited until it was closed behind me before I ran down the hall, up the stairs, and into the safety of my room.

Chapter Four

LITTLE DID I know that the exchange with Lex in the hot tub would be the last time I saw him for weeks. That night, I slept like a rock and got up the next morning sore from sleeping in the same position for so long. I wandered downstairs to find Donna and Conner drinking coffee in the kitchen, both dressed for work. Shit, it was Monday. I had completely forgotten.

I went to the coffeemaker and made myself a cup, still dressed in my robe, my hair in a wild disarray of curls.

Donna eyed me closely. "Sleep well?" she asked, her gaze on my wild hair.

I shoved the mass over my shoulder, pretending to be completely oblivious. I half hoped Lex would see me in this state and change his mind about whatever crazy plans he had for me.

"Yes," I answered, adding sugar and cream to my coffee.

Conner gave me a knowing grin, which I resolutely ignored, and left the kitchen. Donna waited a good thirty seconds after he left to speak.

"So what did you and Lex talk about last night? What did you say to him?" she hissed quietly.

I shrugged and sipped my coffee. "Nothing important," I lied. "Why?"

"Because he left before daylight this morning. He came to our room and spoke with Conner out in the hall for a few minutes, then he just left."

At her words, my heart, my traitorous, idiotic heart, clenched. "What?"

She just looked at me.

I set my own coffee cup down. "He left?"

Donna nodded.

I forced myself to pick up my mug and drink more coffee as though this news didn't affect me in the slightest. Donna obviously saw right through my act, but I was grateful that she didn't say anything.

Instead, she changed the subject. "So what are you doing to-day?" she asked.

I didn't want to talk about this either, but it was a safer topic than Alexander Dimitriades.

"I have some work to do from home, then I need to start the process of finding another place to live."

Because I was such a basket case after the attack, I had taken so much time off of work that I didn't have enough money coming in to keep the apartment I rented. Yet another reason Donna insisted I stay with her and her fiancé. I was slowly getting back into the swing of things, though I was still working mostly part time. I knew I couldn't do it forever and having more money meant moving out and getting some distance between Lex and I. I needed it, for the sake of my sanity and my hormones.

"Are you sure you won't stay for a little while longer?" Donna asked.

"It may be a while before I find a place, Dee. Don't worry, I won't clear out without talking to you first."

She nodded, though I could tell she wanted to argue. I was saved from further discussion by Conner coming back into the kitchen.

"Ready, Donna?" he asked.

She nodded and went to put her coffee cup in the sink. The look she gave me said that she wasn't finished talking about this. I ignored it and waved good-bye to her and Conner as they left the kitchen. He grinned at me as they walked out. For some reason, the damn vampire thought I was hilarious.

I shook my head and set about making myself something to eat. Once I finished my bagel and coffee, I went upstairs to shower and get down to work.

That had been eight weeks ago. In that time, I had started working more and found an apartment. It was smaller than my previous place, but it was much safer. The complex was gated and had a guard at the front. I also had three deadbolts and a chain on my door. Though a vampire could probably just kick it off its hinges, at least I would have protection from human predators.

Also, in those eight weeks, I hadn't heard a peep from Lex. I assumed he finally decided that the measly human, me, wasn't worth the effort, and moved on. I told myself that I was glad, that I didn't want a sexy vampire with dark eyes and phenomenal body chasing after me. I didn't need someone so bossy in my life.

It was early evening on Thursday and I was leaving a meeting with a client when it happened. The sun was low in the sky and I was digging in my bag for my keys. I was a few feet from my car when a small woman approached me.

I nodded in greeting and kept walking. She stopped right in front of me and I started to sidestep her, thinking that she was being rude.

Even though she was the rude one, I muttered, "Excuse me," with a hint of sarcasm and moved to skirt around her.

"Wait," she whispered.

Against my will, my body stopped. Oh shit, not again. I looked up from my purse into her eyes, which were a brilliant hazel, glowing like two amber stones in the setting sun.

"Come with me," she murmured softly.

She turned and began to walk to a large white SUV with dark tinted windows. My feet moved, even as I fought against it with every ounce of will I possessed. I glared at her, hatred in my eyes, as she opened the back passenger door for me. She gestured for me to get in, which I did, and then slammed the door. I tried to turn my head to watch her walk around the vehicle, but she made me sit perfectly still.

There was a male vampire in the front seat, smirking at me. If he hadn't had such cold, dead black eyes and a cruel smile on his face, he would have been beautiful. I refused to meet his eyes as the female vamp opened the door directly behind the driver's seat and climbed into the SUV next to me.

"Look at me," she said.

Like some sort of doll in a horror movie, my head turned on my neck. Though I could slow down my body's response to her commands, I couldn't resist completely. The sharp edge of the memory of my repeated nightmares cut into my composure, but I couldn't scream or cry as I wanted to. Instead, all I could manage was to face the woman who had essentially kidnapped me.

Her eyes were blank, not cold, not angry, as she studied me. Finally, after what seemed like minutes, she merely said, "Sleep."

That was the last thing I remembered.

✧   ✧   ✧

I WOKE UP feeling well-rested and relaxed for the first time in months. I stretched my arms, arching my back. Sunlight filtered in through my blinds in my bedroom. I glanced at the clock and saw it was just a little after six in the morning.

With a sigh, I rolled out of bed. I looked down and realized I was dressed in my prettiest satin nightgown, the one I bought in hopes that it would inspire some passion in Stanley. It hadn't worked and I had shoved it in the back of my lingerie drawer. Instead, I usually wore huge men's t-shirts to bed and baggy shorts. Sometimes a big nightshirt.

I couldn't remember putting it on, but, for some reason, that didn't bother me. Instead, I went into the bathroom, slid off the gown, and climbed into the shower. It was Friday and I had made plans with Donna and several of my other friends to meet for girls' night in at Donna's McMansion. I couldn't wait. Conner was supposed to be gone for the night. There was even talk of a sleepover in the huge home theater. Instead of chairs, though there were a few, Conner had installed huge comfy couches and daybeds. I honestly thought perhaps he hosted orgies in there before he met Donna, but I didn't mention it.

I got ready for work and packed a small bag just in case girls' night in led to drunken merriment and a sleepover. I even included my bathing suit. I had really enjoyed my last girls' night with Donna in the hot tub before Lex showed up.

I floated through my work day, feeling less stressed than usual. I was excited about my weekend plans and I couldn't wait to leave, but I wasn't restless, which was strange. Usually, when I had fun weekend plans, I was full of energy and couldn't sit still. I fidgeted through meetings and work. Today, I just did what needed to be done, oddly calm and serene.

I chalked it up to a good night's sleep. When the clock hit five, I closed down my computer, grabbed my stuff, and headed out to my car. The drive to Donna's took longer than usual because traffic was horrendous. When I finally arrived, I wasn't quite as relaxed as before. Still, it wasn't anything a glass of wine couldn't fix.

I grabbed my stuff and climbed out of the car. Donna threw open the door as I climbed the steps.

"C'mon, bitch. Get a move on! I need a drink!"

I laughed as I followed her inside the house and we made a beeline for the kitchen. She had several bottles of liquor and mixers on the counter top and glasses. On the island, Donna had arranged several trays of food that looked incredible.

I glanced at her in disbelief. "You made that?" I asked.

She glared at me. "What, you don't think I could?"

My eyes shifted away from hers as I tried to figure out the best way to tell her that I certainly did not but still not hurt her feelings. I was saved from answering by the clatter of heels from the hallway.

Shannon, Ricki, and Kerry burst into the kitchen.

"No, it doesn't," Kerry said.

"It does," Ricki insisted.

Shannon was holding her phone in front of the three of them. "Sorry, Kerry, I'm with Ricki, it kinda does."

"What are you three arguing about?" I asked, grateful for the interruption and the protection of the three of them.

Shannon handed me her phone.

"Oh sweet baby Jesus!" I shouted and tried to give it back to her. "What the hell is that?"

"It's uncut peen," Ricki answered.

"What?" I asked, trying not to look at the screen, but failing. It was like a car crash. You couldn't look away, even though you really, really wanted to.

Kerry sighed. "It's an uncircumcised penis," she answered matter-of-factly. "And I don't see what the big deal is. It isn't a common practice in countries like Great Britain unless you're Jewish. It's natural."

"It looks like a fucking Chinese finger trap, that's why," Ricki cried.

Shannon just snorted. I bit my lip to keep from laughing, because, while Kerry had a point, Ricki's description was spot on and hilarious.

Kerry looked at Donna. "Help me out here, please."

Shannon and Ricki looked at Donna in confusion for a moment and I realized what Kerry meant. I couldn't hold in the guffaw that burst out of me and clapped my hand over my mouth.

"What?" Ricki asked.

"Think about it," I managed to say between giggles.

Finally, the light dawned for Ricki and Shannon.

"Oh my God!" Ricki shrieked. "Does Conner have a Chinese finger trap?"

The rest of us, with the exception of Donna, dissolved into laughter. Donna's face said it all, as a deep red flush crept up her neck to her cheeks.

"Shut up," she snapped as she went back to making drinks. "I'm not discussing the state of Conner's penis with the four of you." She paused, looking confused. "And why are we talking about this at all?"

Shannon snorted. "Those pictures are from a guy I follow on Twitter. He's constantly posting pics of his junk."

This set us off again and it was at least five minutes before we were able to calm down. By then, Donna had mixed up a huge batch of mojitos and was watching us with a perturbed expression on her face.

I wiped the tears from my eyes. "Sorry, Dee. You have to admit it was a little funny."

She made a face, but kept drinking.

I decided to let the subject drop, as did the other girls. It wasn't nice to laugh at another woman's peen. Or at the peen of her fiancé.

I saw the corner of Donna's mouth twitch and realized she caught that last errant thought. She hadn't completely lost her sense of humor.

"So who made the food?" Shannon asked.

Donna set her glass down with a sharp snap. "Goddammit, is it so unbelievable that I could cook something like that?"

Kerry and Ricki both nodded.

Donna threw her hands in the air. "Fine. No, I didn't cook it. Mrs. Brown, the housekeeper, did."

I walked over and took a glass of mojito from the counter in front of her. When her eyes met mine, I winked. She just shook her head, but smiled. We lived to give each other shit in our group. If we weren't ragging on one another, that usually meant someone was sick, hurt, or we were fighting like sisters.

We all snacked and drank and discussed our week. It was nice to hang out. Now that things were more settled between Donna and Conner, we tried to have girls' night in at least twice a month, though we usually had it at her house because it was so much larger and nicer than anything we had on our own. Kerry's condo was pretty damn cool, as was Ricki's loft and Shannon's apartment, but putting the five of us in any of those spaces was a tight fit.

Finally, after we cleaned the platters and stuck them in the sink, we took our booze and headed toward the hot tub. I brought my bag and purse with me so I could change into my suit.

Everyone changed and we all sat in the hot, bubbling water, sipping our drinks, and chatting quietly. It was incredibly relaxing. I felt the last of the tension caused by the earlier traffic jams finally ease. I leaned my head back against the side of the tub and just breathed.

It was going on ten at night when Donna perked up.

"Conner's home," she squealed.

She was definitely tipsy, which meant that she had consumed a lot of alcohol. Vampires had to drink much more than an average human in order to get drunk. Or drink blood from someone who was two drinks away from alcohol poisoning. I glanced at the table near the hot tub and saw two empty bottles of rum. Shit, we were all hammered.

I climbed out of the water and was standing by the table, pouring myself one last mojito, when Conner walked into the room. All the girls, with the exception of Donna and I, whistled and catcalled as he walked toward his fiancée.

I could understand why. He moved with loose-hipped grace that was emphasized by his snug dark wash jeans and tight black t-shirt.

As he leaned down to kiss her, the noise intensified. When he straightened to grin at the girls, I swear they all moaned and he just chuckled.

"Okay, bitches, this is killing me. I need more booze," Ricki said loudly. She pointed to Kerry and Shannon. "You two come help me make some more mojitos or margaritas or something."

Conner and Donna grinned at them as they left the room.

I realized that I had somehow ended up over by my bag. I glanced around, wondering how in the hell I had moved without realizing it. A little voice whispered almost silently in my mind. I stopped what I was doing for a moment, trying to catch what the voice said, but couldn't quite grasp it all.

In horror, I watched as my hands began to move without my permission. My left hand opened my purse and my right reached inside. I tried to stop myself, to control the motions of my hands, but they seemed to have a mind of their own. Literally.

I tried to say something, to scream for help, but no sound came out. Instead, I watched as my right hand emerged from the bag, wrapped around the grip of a snub-nosed revolver. I wasn't even sure what kind of gun it was. Only that it was big and scary looking.

I told my fingers to release the handle, but my feet carried me toward Conner and Donna. As I moved across the room, I realized that I was about to harm one of the people I cared for the most. I opened my mouth, but nothing came out. A vague memory of a female vampire with hazel eyes skirted the edge of my mind, but refused to come into focus.

Donna and Conner were talking to Ricki, Kerry, and Shannon and they were laughing and smiling, completely oblivious to the danger I presented. I struggled to force enough air to scream past the tightness in my throat, but nothing happened.

God, I was going to shoot my best friend and her fiancé in cold blood. Sweat broke out on my skin as I fought the hold of the vampire mind control. I was slowing down my movements, but still couldn't gain complete control.

I realized that there was nothing I could do, physically, to stop what I was about to do. Then, it hit me. I didn't have to say anything aloud. While the mind control and brainwashing controlled my body, my mind was still clear.

In my head, as loud as I could, I screamed, *Conner!*

It worked.

His head snapped up and twisted so he could see me. When he saw the gun I held in my hand and the sweat pouring from my forehead, he immediately understood what was happening.

Help me! I begged silently.

Moving so quickly that my eyes couldn't track him, Conner crossed the room and grabbed my wrist.

"I'm sorry," he whispered. Then his free hand came up and he clocked me with his palm.

At his open-handed slap, I went down hard. All I could think is that at least it hadn't been his fist, because that fucking hurt, then all the lights went out.

Chapter Five

SOMETHING ROUGH MOVED lightly across my cheek. I twitched, trying to dislodge it, but it continued on a path across my cheekbone, up my temple, and into my hair. I realized that someone's hand was in my hair, gently massaging my scalp and running fingers through the strands. It felt incredibly nice. Without a thought, I turned my face into the caress, enjoying the sensation of being petted.

Then my memory returned and my eyes popped open. I started to jack knife into a sitting position, but a firm hand on my breast-bone held me flat.

"Sh, little one. Don't try to sit up just yet. Give yourself a moment."

My eyes rolled around until I could see Lex sitting next to my hip, wearing a dark red shirt and gray slacks. He looked edible.

"Is Conner okay? Donna? I didn't hurt them, did I?" I asked. "Oh God, what about the other girls? Did they see?"

Lex shook his head. "They weren't in the room when Conner took you down."

I tried to sit up again.

Lex continued to stroke my hair. "Calm down, Ivie. It's fine. You did not have a chance to harm them." He turned my head slightly so that the left side of my face was in the light. "I'm more concerned about you. Conner said he hit you a little harder than he normally would have. He wanted to be sure you were unconscious."

I blinked and took stock of my body. Other than a slight headache and the pain in my cheek, I felt fine. "I think I'm good," I murmured.

I gingerly pushed myself into sitting position and looked around. I didn't recognize my surroundings. Touching my cheek and feeling the tightness and swelling under my skin, I winced.

"Where am I?" I asked.

Lex pushed my hand away and touched his lips to the place where Conner's slap had connected.

I froze and stared at him as he straightened and stood from the lounger I had been lying on. I completely lost track of my question because I was so consumed with the hot imprint of his mouth on my cheek.

"You're at my home," he answered shortly.

"Huh?" I asked. Then I blinked and remembered that I had asked him where I was. I watched as he walked to a small bar area in the corner of the room and poured me a glass of water from a bottle. "Why am I here?"

"For your safety," was his only answer.

I stared at him for a moment before I responded. I didn't like the way he was avoiding my gaze or the way that he wasn't giving me any more information than necessary. I didn't like it at all.

"What do you mean, *for my safety*?" I asked.

He came back to the chaise lounge and handed me the water. "Drink that."

I took the glass, but just held it and stared at him.

"Drink," he said again, his voice dropping.

God, he was so damned bossy. I wished that I didn't find that attractive.

I took a couple of small sips. "Are you going to answer my question?"

"After your actions at Conner's home, it has become clear that our enemies intend to use whatever means necessary to obtain what they want, even if the means are dishonorable."

"Okay, what exactly happened?" He looked at me incredulously, and I clarified. "I mean, I know what I did. I didn't want to do it, but couldn't stop myself. I've only felt that way one other time in my life and that was when I was kidnapped a few months ago. Obviously, a vampire brainwashed me, or hypnotized me or something."

Lex nodded. "Yes. We are unsure who the culprit was, but it seems that someone among our kind decided to make a preemptive strike and remove Conner from the equation permanently."

Now I was even more confused than before. "What do you mean, *remove Conner from the equation permanently?* What equation? Why would anyone want to hurt Donna or Conner?"

Sighing heavily, he came and sat down next to me again, much too closely. I moved back slightly so there was a small amount of space between us. I wasn't ready for him to touch me again just yet. Along with my memory of the night before, I also remembered that he had disappeared for two months.

"There are things happening among vampire kind right now. Things I can't share with you just yet. I will, and soon, but now is not the time. All I can tell you right now, is that Conner and his position on the Council are very important to the machinations of those we are opposing."

I wanted to roll my eyes at his evasions, but managed to refrain. His secrecy seemed a little over the top. It wasn't like the

Antichrist had been born or we were on our way to becoming a nuclear wasteland. Vampires were squabbling, probably over something not so important to humans. I mean, it wasn't like they ran the world.

"What are you thinking about?" he asked.

I schooled my features, realizing that my thoughts would probably piss him off. I wanted to lie, but his reaction to my previous lies made me hesitant to do so again. Instead, I went with a partial truth.

"Just wondering what this is all about." My words were innocuous and neutral and completely true. They just weren't the entirety of my thoughts on the matter.

Lex stared at me intently for a moment and I wondered if he was poking around in my head. He had promised never to do so without my permission, though why I would ever give it to him, I didn't know.

"What?" I asked defensively. "Are you trying to read my mind?"

Lex shook his head. "No. Actually, I'm trying not to read your mind. You broadcast your thoughts rather loudly. It takes an effort to block you from my own."

I blushed. "Sorry, I'm not used to censoring *my private thoughts*," I said sarcastically. "I'll get used to it in time."

He smirked a little at my sarcasm. "Watch it, Ivie. Don't push me too far."

I shivered at the dark promise in his words. Somehow, I had the feeling that too far would be just far enough for me to skate along the thin edge of pleasure and pain in the most delicious way possible. As soon as I realized what I was thinking, I cursed inwardly and controlled my wayward hormones.

"Back to the subject at hand, I can't tell you what is happening right now, but I will very soon. There are decisions to be made, plans to be set in motion. Once that is done, I can answer most, if not all, of your questions."

I nodded. I decided that I was ready to try standing. My head still ached a bit, but I desperately needed the bathroom.

Slowly, I turned and placed my feet on the floor next to the chaise. With the care of someone aged or infirm, I raised myself into a standing position. In a flash, Lex was standing next to me, hands on my arms.

"Easy," he murmured.

I waited a moment until my legs were solid beneath me then gently pulled away. "I'm good. I just need to know where the bathroom is."

A small smile crossed Lex's mouth and he turned. "Go down the hall, second door on your left."

"Thanks." I moved as quickly as my shaky legs could carry me.

A few minutes later, my pressing need was gone and I'd washed my face and hands thoroughly. I returned to the large den, taking in Lex's opulent home. The walls were all painted in warm neutrals and there was artwork scattered throughout the rooms I passed. Lex obviously appreciated art and antiques. From what I could see, his home was full of them.

I went back into the den where Lex was waiting for me.

He studied me as I entered the room. "Better?"

I nodded. Crossing my arms over my torso, I tucked them tight against me. I was fairly certain I was alone in this huge house with Lex. I felt vulnerable and nervous.

"Well, I guess I should get home. I have a lot to do before I go back to work on Monday," I said. I tried to appear casual as I glanced around the floor for my shoes.

Quietly, Lex responded, "Ivie, we should talk."

I pulled my hair away from my face, becoming a little more intent on my search. I didn't see my shoes or my purse anywhere and all I was wearing was my swimsuit and a robe. After my last chat with him, I knew I probably wouldn't want to listen to what he had to say.

I watched as Lex crossed to a matched pair of sofas and sat. He gestured to the seat next to him. Unwilling to bend, I intentionally sat on the couch that faced him. His face tightened slightly, but he said nothing. I realized it was probably childish, but the closer our proximity, the fuzzier my thinking. I needed space between us in order for my brain to function properly. And I had a sinking feeling I would need all my wits about me for this conversation.

Lex began speaking, jarring me out of my thoughts. "I'm sure you already understand that you are not as safe as we believed."

Cautiously, I nodded. This was true. It was clear the bad guys thought they could use me for their own ends.

"Well, Conner, Donna, and I discussed, at length, the best way to keep you safe," he continued. At his obvious hesitancy and words, that sinking feeling turned into a hundred foot drop. I wasn't going to like what came next. "We think it's best if you stay with me for a while, until things are settled."

I was right. I didn't like it. Immediately, I shook my head. "No way. No how. Not gonna happen," I responded.

His eyes began to brighten in a way that was both scary and beautiful. As though someone had flipped a switch inside of him. I witnessed these changes in other vampires before and I knew it didn't bode well for the rest of our talk.

"What?" he asked in a low, dangerous tone.

I crossed my arms over my chest, fighting the shiver of dread that trailed down my spine. "Conner pulled this shit with Donna and she never moved out. She's also still in danger. I refuse to be trapped in a house with you indefinitely." I paused. "I'll be more careful and I'll go back to working from home most of the time."

It was Lex's turn to shake his head. "That's unacceptable."

I scowled at him. "I live in a gated apartment complex." It was a flimsy argument, but I did not want to live with Lex. I knew it wouldn't be long before I was a vamp tramp. I wouldn't be able to resist him.

His eyes grew brighter and angrier. "Any newborn vampire could coerce or force someone to let them in and gain entry to your flat. You will stay here."

"Fine. You're right. It's not safe at my place." His face relaxed slightly until I continued. "I'll ask Donna if I can stay with her."

Lex looked angrier than before. "I won't allow that and neither will Conner."

I scoffed. "You don't get to *allow* or *disallow* me to do anything, Lex. You are not my boss, my father, or my boyfriend. And I would even tell them to go screw themselves if they tried to make me move in with them against my will." I shot to my feet, seriously considering walking in bare feet back to my fucking apartment if I had to. "Oh, and you forget, Donna lives with Conner now. You may be used to women who simper and do as they're told, but you and Conner are in for a rude awakening if you think that she'll go along with forcing me to live with you."

Also, I hadn't forgotten that he'd made quite an effort to get me worked up and then disappeared for two months. No way in hell was I mentioning that.

Lex rose, towering over me. "Do not test me on this, Ivie. You will not win," he said. I knew it was a threat, just like I knew he wouldn't actually hurt me. I wasn't sure why I believed it, but I did.

"I can't stay here," I stated again. "I'll feel like a prisoner. At least at Donna's, I feel more like I'm visiting than trapped." I couldn't stop the wobble in my voice. I despised the weakness, but I couldn't prevent it.

Lex cocked his head and studied me for a moment. His eyes began to return to their usual dark brown. "I understand, little one. I will call Conner and he will take you back to his home."

I hated the disappointment on his face and in his words. Then I hated myself for giving a damn. Why couldn't I keep my emotional distance from this man? I sank back down on the sofa as he pulled his cell phone from his pocket and left the room. Hugging myself, I waited for him to complete his call and come back.

I waited for a good long while. Just as I gathered the courage to leave the room and go looking for Lex, he returned, tucking his phone back in his pocket.

His gaze moved over me from the top of my head to my toes, concern in his eyes. "I will drive you to Conner's now."

I pulled my lower lip between my teeth and nodded. He didn't say another word, only gestured for me to follow him. Within five minutes I was in the passenger seat of his Audi, and we were pulling out of the driveway. I glanced back at the house as Lex drove away and had to force myself not to gape. His home was just as large, if not larger, than Conner's.

He also lived close to Conner. The drive took only ten minutes. When he pulled up in front of the house, I climbed out of the car, heading toward the front door. I realized he wasn't next to me and glanced over my shoulder. This time I couldn't stop my mouth from falling open. He pulled a duffel and a garment bag out of his backseat and shut the door.

"What are you doing?" I asked.

"Getting my things."

That was both an answer and a non-answer to my question. I sighed and leveled my eyes at him, meeting his stare full-on. It was difficult because his eyes carried the weight of several lifetimes. I'd never realized before now that his eyes gave away his age. Even though he appeared to be in his mid-to-late thirties, his eyes showed every year he existed.

I put both hands on my hips and took a stance my mother used on me when I was keeping things from her. It always worked for her, so I was hoping it would do the same for me.

"I'm not moving until you tell me why you have enough luggage to stay for at least a week," I said.

Lex stopped on the step below me, but he was still a couple of inches taller than me, the bastard. "Because I am staying here. With you."

Chapter Six

A FEW SECONDS AFTER Lex dropped that little bombshell, Donna threw the front door open and reached out to drag me into the house by my arm.

I whirled on her. "No. Just no," I said, my voice high.

She looked confused. "What are you talking about, Ivie? I don't understand. I thought you wanted to stay here."

I glanced over my shoulder and saw Lex watching me with an inscrutable expression on his face.

"Please excuse us," I said haughtily. I snatched the sleeve of Donna's shirt and dragged her all the way through the house to the veranda in the back. Once we were outside, I led her another twenty feet away from the house. Then I dropped her arm, stood extremely close to her, and whispered, "I cannot stay here if Lex is under the same roof."

She blinked at me. "What?"

I huffed out a breath and pinched the bridge of my nose. The mild headache I had been experiencing earlier was now a full-blown, *my head is in a vice* monstrosity.

"Dee, please keep up. I cannot stay here if he's here. That man freaks me the fuck out!" I was almost shouting when I finished my sentence.

She pulled me into a hug, patting my back gently. "Are you afraid he's going to hurt you?" she asked. "I know he looks really scary and acts that way most of the time, but he's really a good guy. He just wants to protect you."

I laughed, but it was short and completely devoid of sincere humor. "I feel like a particularly juicy steak must when it's dangling a few feet above a Doberman who hasn't been fed in a week." I closed my eyes and pressed my forehead to her shoulder. "He doesn't scare me. I'm scared of the way he makes me feel," I whispered brokenly.

Donna pushed me back gently so she could see my face. "How does he make you feel?" she asked.

I licked my lips. "He makes me want things I know are bad for me."

"How so?" she asked.

I wanted to laugh. She was using what I thought of as her 'shrink' voice. Whenever she wanted to get to the bottom of one of the girls' personal problems, she would ask probing questions. And, I'll be damned, but she usually got to the crux of the problem every time. The only obstacle this time is that I didn't want to tell her that I wanted to stay human. I knew that she wouldn't show it, but it would hurt her feelings if she believed I thought less of her for becoming a vampire. Honestly, I was glad Conner turned her. If he hadn't, she'd be dead. But that wasn't what I wanted for myself.

I didn't think less of her, but most vampires, including Conner and Lex, thought less of me because I was human. I knew Donna didn't share their feelings. She was too new, but I worried that she would one day.

"He's very controlling," I said.

She nodded. "Most vampires his age are. He was a powerful man when he was turned. He's used to everyone, man or woman, jumping to do his bidding."

I shrugged off her answer. "It's more than that, Dee. I think he likes to be in control in all things…" I trailed off then sighed when she didn't catch my drift. "I think he's into kink, okay?" I snapped.

"Oh!" Donna's mouth rounded into an 'O' and her cheeks turned pink. Then she hummed in the back of her throat. "That's kind of hot."

"Fuck me," I muttered under my breath.

She poked me in the shoulder. "Don't pretend you don't like it. I've seen the books on your Kindle, bitch. You love it."

I nodded. "I know, but I'm not sure he'd be good for me. I mean, why me? I'm just human."

Shit, shit, shit. I hadn't meant to say that. It just slipped out. I watched as the light bulb clicked on.

She leaned in closer to me. "Listen, Ivie, I don't think you understand…"

"Donna?" Conner's voice interrupted our conversation. "Is there a reason you and Ivie are whispering in the backyard while Alexander is still standing in the foyer?"

I closed my eyes, wondering how much Conner heard. Then I straightened and turned to look at him. "Sorry, Conner. I had a girl problem. Donna was just giving me a hand."

Donna walked around me, rolling her eyes. "Don't apologize to him, Ivie. He'll think I actually care about manners." She smirked at her fiancé. "Lex has been to our house quite a bit since I moved in and I don't remember him waiting at the door like a child before."

Conner tried to appear stern, but I could see the smile he was fighting. "You should be a better hostess, lass."

"Whatever," she replied. Donna turned and pointed at me. "You and I will finish our discussion later tonight."

I opened my mouth to try and talk my way out of it, but she just shook her head and tisked at me.

"No. I will talk about it and you will listen," she stated firmly.

I sighed and followed her into the house.

✧   ✧   ✧

LATER THAT NIGHT, I was saved from continuing the conversation with Donna. She received an important work call from California around nine and locked herself in the study to deal with whatever emergency prompted the after-hours call. I was ensconced in my room by ten.

For some reason, Donna had given me a different guest room than before. I didn't question it because the room was just as large and beautiful as the one I had stayed in previously. I took a leisurely bath in the huge, jetted tub in the bathroom and then stretched out on the fabulous mattress with my Kindle to read before I went to sleep.

Donna was right. I did have a lot of BDSM-themed books on my eReader. In fact, I was in the middle of reading a series by an author that I adored. Her female characters might be submissive, but they were strong, fun, and real. And the sex was, well, phenomenal and off-the-charts hot.

It was midnight before I finished the book I was reading and finally decided to try and sleep. I was incredibly turned on, but didn't dare do anything about it with three vampires in the house. Especially since one in particular might decide to come offer me a hand...or something else.

As a result, it was almost 2 a.m. before I fell asleep. Immediately, I sank into a luscious dream. A large, muscled form slid into the bed behind me. At first, strong arms held me close, cuddling me. I moaned softly and snuggled closer, glad to have the contact, even if it was in my subconscious. When my ass came into contact with his hips, he growled low in his throat. Hot, rough hands began to move, over the huge men's t-shirt I wore to bed, then under it. God, it was the most delicious dream I'd had in a long time.

I arched my back, grinding my bottom into the hips behind me, moaning in appreciation when I felt his erection. Then I gasped as strong, callused fingers plucked my nipples firmly. My entire body went taut. I reached behind me and sank my fingers into the hair at the nape of his neck. As he played with my nipples, I began to whimper. When he lifted a hand to cover my mouth and muffle the sounds coming from me, I nipped his fingers.

His body went completely rigid. "Christ," he muttered before his hard hand grasped my chin and turned my face toward his.

As soon as our mouths touched, his teeth sank lightly into my lip. It was then that I realized I wasn't dreaming, that this entire situation was all too real. My eyes flew open and I leapt from the bed. I looked around and realized the room was empty. My body throbbed and my heart was hammering. It felt so intense, so real. How could it have just been a dream?

I sank down on the edge of the mattress, trying to control the wild beating of my heart and my shallow pants. Holy shit, if real life sex with Alexander Dimitriades was anything like dream sex, I would never be able to say no to him. Okay, so it was dream foreplay, but I knew exactly where that dream was heading and we weren't going to have tea and cookies.

Once I was certain my legs would hold me, I staggered into the bathroom and splashed cold water on my hot, flushed face. I looked at my shell-shocked expression in the mirror and had to smile. A vampire wet dream might have been just as stressful as the dreams I had of the vamp that had kidnapped me, but they were still preferable. I'd take sexual frustration over terror any day.

I realized that reading a very sexy book before bed might not have been the best idea. Especially with a sex-on-a-stick vampire a few doors down who made it very clear he wanted to, as Kerry called it, go spelunking in my lady cave. Just thinking of the ridiculous terms for sex my girlfriends came up with helped calm my raging hormones. Spelunking didn't sound like a sexy pastime.

After I dried my damp face, I wandered back into the bedroom and climbed into bed. As I burrowed under the covers, I couldn't stop thinking of Lex and the way he made me feel. Between the book I had been reading earlier and that dream, I had gone way beyond hot and bothered, straight into nuclear meltdown.

With an aggravated sigh, I rolled over and punched my pillow into submission, trying to get comfortable. It had been too long since I'd had decent sex or an orgasm with an actual living, breathing partner. Stanley wasn't a huge dud like Donna and my girlfriends made him out to be. We may not have had insane, mind-blowing, gorilla sex, but he always took care of me. It was nice. Comfortable.

The thought of sex with Lex, which made me smile because it rhymed, wasn't nice or comfortable. It was consuming, terrifying. That man could chew me up and spit me out and not just because he was a vampire. I fell asleep thinking that I would enjoy the ride, even if I ended up mangled by the end of it.

Light seeped around the edges of the drapes in my room when I woke. Stretching slowly, I relished feeling warm and cozy. God, the beds at Donna's house were so much better than mine. Then I realized why I felt so comfortable. A long, muscled arm was wrapped around my waist and a furnace pressed lightly against my back. My sleepy stretches stopped and my entire body got tight. What the hell?

I must have said that out loud, because the arm around my waist tightened. I tried to scramble to the edge of the bed, but I only succeeded in rolling onto my back and getting stuck like a turtle, arms and legs waving wildly in my attempt to escape.

"Let me go," I snapped, trying to toss my hair out of my face.

"Calm down," Lex said sternly.

I glared at him through the thick veil of my curly hair. "What the hell are you doing in here?" I demanded.

He held me easily. "Calm down before you hurt yourself, Ivie."

I stopped fighting, mostly because he was as immovable as a three ton boulder. I stared daggers at him and tried to blow my hair out of my face.

"Are you going to answer my question?" I asked in the coldest voice I could muster.

Lex sighed as though he were equal parts frustrated and disappointed. I didn't care for that sigh. Not because I found it annoying, which I did, but because I also didn't like the way it made me feel. I shouldn't give a shit if I frustrated or disappointed this man.

"You called me."

My brows snapped together. "Excuse me? How could I call you if I was *sleeping*?" I hissed.

Lex turned me to face him and rolled so he was on his back. I was distracted by the wide expanse of olive skin and dusting of hair that I quickly realized was his bare chest. I knew he was a big guy, but I didn't realize how big until just now, since I was practically lying on top of him. I lifted a hand to push him away, but forgot what I intended to do as soon as my fingertips touched skin. Heat radiated off him, as though a fire were burning beneath his skin. The skin across his ribs was smooth, firm, and stretched over taut muscle.

"I'm not sure," he answered, breaking my hot guy trance.

"What? How can you not know?"

Lex looked a little uncomfortable. "It's never happened before. Usually, humans can't *call* a vampire telepathically. You can broadcast your thoughts, share images, but the ability to summon a vampire is rare."

"I don't understand," I said. I relaxed, completely forgetting about Lex's naked chest, resting my weight against him.

He brushed my hair out of my face, absentmindedly playing with the strands, as he stared across the room. It was as if he were a million miles away. "When you called me, Ivie, I felt as though I *had* to come. It is a bit like how a vampire controls a human. We can call them to us, it's part of our abilities as predators to aid us in trapping prey." I shivered at his description after having been on the receiving end of that particular trait before, but he only held me closer as he continued. "I could have resisted you, but it would have been difficult." His eyes returned to me, intense. "And I didn't particularly want to resist. Especially after that delectable dream you shared with me."

I gasped, feeling the blood rush to my face. I knew I was beet red. "You know about my dream?" I asked softly.

His mouth quirked slightly, but his eyes were hot and dark, promising me that the things I dreamed were only the beginning. "Yes. Somehow I think you pulled me into the dream with you. I was in control of my actions, yet I had no memory of how I got in your room. That's never happened to me before."

I was silent, trying to decide what to say. I wasn't sure what I even could say. Mortification overwhelmed any ability I had to think. I couldn't believe that the dream hadn't been real, yet it also had, in a way.

I decided to move away from the intimate details and focus on his previous words. "Is it rare for a human to be able to share dreams with a vampire?" I asked.

He nodded, his face serious. "It is extremely rare."

I wasn't sure what I thought, so I just kept my mouth shut. Lex continued to study me for a few more moments.

Finally, he spoke, "I can see that this is overwhelming for you. I think it's best if we discuss it further after you've had breakfast."

I almost snorted at his understatement. Overwhelming? The concept he presented was well beyond overwhelming. I knew next to nothing about vampires, other than the fact that they had fangs, drank blood, and had the ability to control minds. I would have to think about it later, after caffeine. As for discussing it further, I would be doing that. But not with Lex. Right now, he had me trapped, but, as soon as I was free, all bets were off. I intended to go back to avoiding him as best I could.

Suddenly, his face grew tense. "I'm not reading your thoughts, but I can read your face. You will not avoid this conversation, Ivie. Am I understood?"

I stared down at him, my eyes wide. While the independent woman that usually ruled my brain told me to kick him in the nuts, there was another part of me that melted at his demand. The same part that hated it when he looked disappointed or angry with me. My tummy felt like a bowl of Jell-O. I swallowed hard and nodded.

"Say it," he said sternly.

I wasn't sure what he wanted me to say, but I was also afraid to ask. His gaze softened slightly, as though he understood my predicament perfectly.

"Say 'I understand', Ivie," he prompted.

Though it was difficult for me to hold back my bratty response of 'I understand, Ivie', I did. Instead, I merely said, "I understand."

He nodded and pressed a light kiss to my forehead. Then he released me, rolled off the bed, and headed toward the door that led out to the hall. I blinked at his gorgeous, naked back and his firm ass in his navy pajama pants, then he was gone.

I flopped back into the fluffy pillows on the bed and stared at the ceiling, wondering what in the fuck had just happened. I had gone to bed alone the night before, shared foreplay in a dream, and woken up to find a man in my bed. Screw all those romance novels on my Kindle, I had enough stuff happening in my own life to write one of my own.

Chapter Seven

AFTER THE STRANGE encounter in my room earlier that morning, I expected Lex to be waiting on me when I came down for breakfast an hour later. He wasn't. In fact, he was locked in the study with Conner. Donna had gone in to work under the watchful eye of one of Conner's men. I didn't know his name, probably because I was afraid to speak to him. His eyes were pale amber and cold, like a wolf's. Anytime he looked at me, I felt as though he could see straight through to my soul and it didn't impress him.

I ate a quick breakfast, gulped a huge cup of coffee, and decided to try and work. Maybe if I appeared to be busy, Lex would leave me alone for a while. I grabbed my laptop from my room and took it into the rarely used library.

I loved Conner's house, because, not only did he have a study, he also had a huge library. It was two stories and full of books and windows. The room was filled with light and escape. I set my laptop up on a large table by a window overlooking the side yard and began going through my office emails. My boss had sent me the specifics on a new project that was due the following week.

My plan was a little too effective. I began working on a project for my graphics firm. I was so immersed in the details of my work that I missed lunch. In fact, the only reason I stopped was due to

Conner's housekeeper, Susan. She came into the room, dust cloth and furniture polish in hand. A few steps inside the door, she hesitated.

"I'm sorry, Ms. Lang. I didn't realize you were still in here." She fidgeted slightly. "Do you want me to come back later?"

I rolled my shoulders, suddenly aware of the knots in my neck and back. "What time is it?" I asked. I could have looked at my computer, but that would have been useless. My eyes were so blurry from the hours of staring at the screen I never would have been able to read the tiny clock in the corner of the screen.

"3 p.m." Susan seemed shocked that I had no clue what time it was.

My eyebrows rose. "Really?" I asked.

She nodded. "Do you want me to come back later?" she asked again.

I shook my head. "No, no, of course not. I need to stop for a while anyway. I've been at this since 8:30 this morning."

Her eyes widened. "Do you want me to make you something to eat?" she asked. "You really shouldn't skip meals, Ms. Lang."

I waved her offer away. "No thank you, Susan. Please call me Ivie. Ms. Lang reminds me too much of my mother." I loved my mom but I didn't necessarily want to be her.

"Okay, Ms. La…I mean, Ivie."

I saved my work and shut down my computer. "I'm going to get out of your way and go stretch my legs."

She murmured something I couldn't understand as I left the room, carrying my laptop and charge cord. I didn't ask her to clarify because I was pretty sure Susan was the shyest person I'd ever met. I just nodded to her as I walked by. She smiled slightly but that was all.

After I deposited my laptop in my room, I slid on a pair of shoes. I knew that Conner would never let me go for a walk in his fabulous neighborhood. I could already hear his sexy Scottish brogue telling me that it was unsafe. I decided to take a stroll around the backyard. Hell, it was almost the size of a city block anyway.

I was just getting ready to head back inside when Donna popped out the back door of the house, still dressed in a sharp dark plum suit, two glasses of white wine in her hands. As I walked under the roof covering the veranda, she gave me one of the glasses and walked over to the swing that Lex and I had shared a few weeks before.

Plopping down hard and causing the swing to sway alarmingly, Donna took a large sip of her wine. "Damn, I had a long day." She turned her eyes to me. "How was yours?" she asked.

I shrugged. "I had a lot of work to do."

Her mouth quirked. "Still avoiding Lex?" I didn't answer right away and she perked up. "What happened?" she asked.

I settled on to the swing beside her and took a drink of my own wine. "Can I have a couple days to process it before we talk it to death?" I asked. Typically, I wanted to discuss this kind of thing with my girlfriends, but Lex had been correct this morning. I was completely overwhelmed by what I was thinking and feeling and all the information would take some time to digest.

Donna watched me carefully for a moment before she sighed. "Yes, but we're doing girls' night in with all the girls when we do talk about it. I have a feeling I'm gonna need Kerry to make me her Man Problem Special."

Kerry's Man Problem Special was basically a shot of tequila chased with a Long Island Iced Tea. Simple, effective, but lethal.

"Fine." I just hoped by then I figured out exactly what was going on inside my own head.

She seemed mollified by my answer and continued to drink her wine without a word. We sat together on the swing for a while in companionable silence. Every now and then, she would use her toe to gently set the swing in motion.

I wasn't sure how long we sat out there together, just enjoying each other's presence when Conner appeared on the veranda, a chilled bottle of white wine in his hand.

"Dinner is almost ready, ladies," he said softly, as he refilled our glasses.

Donna smiled at him, affection and tenderness plain on her face. While Conner's expression wasn't as open, his blue eyes shimmered with love and contentment. I felt my throat tighten as I saw it. I couldn't help the wave of longing that crashed through me. I wanted that. I wanted to come home after a long day and have someone pour me a glass of wine and make me dinner. Or at least help me cook. I wanted to go to bed at night with a man who looked at me the way Conner was looking at Donna.

"Thanks, babe," Donna said softly. Conner just nodded at her, then me, and headed back into the house.

She and I sighed at the same time, though hers was much more dreamy than mine. I gave her a sidelong glance.

"You're a lucky bitch. You know that, right?" I asked.

She snickered and took another sip of her wine. "Yes, I do."

I shook my head and stood. "Well, let's go inside and set the table for dinner."

Donna rose to her feet and we walked into the kitchen together. As it turned out, we didn't need to set the table, Conner had. There were only three place settings. At the sight, I felt my stomach clench with a feeling so alien I couldn't name it.

Conner noticed me looking at the table. "Lex had to go to his club for a few hours. He's having issues with his night manager and I think he's hoping his presence will clue the woman in to the fact that she is fucking up."

I nodded nonchalantly, as though this news didn't send relief coursing through my veins. After Lex's disappearing act, I didn't want to admit how upset I had been at the idea that he had left again for parts unknown. Especially since he hadn't said good-bye to me.

I set those thoughts firmly aside. I didn't need to be thinking like that. When it came to the vampire, Lex, I needed to remain detached, though he seemed intent on making sure that was impossible.

Dinner was great. Conner had made shepherd's pie, my favorite comfort food. I eyed him speculatively after we ate, wondering if he had fished that little piece of information out of my brain.

When he caught me staring at him for the third time in fifteen minutes, Conner sighed and set aside his fork. "Okay, what now?" he asked.

I blushed lightly, but met his gaze squarely. "Did you know shepherd's pie is one of my favorite things?" I asked.

He nodded. "I did. Donna told me."

My blush intensified. I hadn't thought of that. I had just assumed that he took advantage of his abilities because he could. It was embarrassing to realize that I had been so suspicious of my best friend's fiancé. Her fiancé who just wanted to do something nice for me, like make my favorite dinner.

I sent him an apologetic smile. In that uncanny way of his, and Lex's, he seemed to understand what I was thinking and sent me a wink.

After that silent exchange, some of the tension in my belly dissipated. The rest of the meal was actually a lot of fun. I had never realized how witty and sweet Conner really was. His tales of his life before he came to America and the shenanigans he was involved in as a boy in Scotland were funny and bittersweet. I could sense that time had not dimmed his memories or the feeling he had for his friends and family who were now long gone.

I was beginning to understand what Donna meant when she said a lot of vampires were more like humans than monsters. Seeing this side of Conner, I could understand why Donna fell in love with him.

After dinner, I insisted on helping Donna with the dishes. Well, I insisted Donna and I do the dishes. Conner had laughed when he saw the dirty looks my friend was shooting me for volunteering her for the chore.

He walked over to Donna, leaned in, and kissed her lightly on the mouth. "I have some calls to make, lass. Don't kill each other while I'm gone," he admonished.

Donna scoffed and waved him away. "You don't have to worry about what I'll do to her. Worry about the torture she's going to inflict upon me."

I rolled my eyes as I finished clearing the table. "Washing dishes isn't torture. It's a household chore no one really likes, but it's only fair we do them since Conner cooked."

She grumbled about pain in the ass humans and fiancés who used every dish in the house to make a single meal, but she helped. It was after eight when we finished drying the last dish and putting them away.

"Thanks, babe," she said, folding the dish towel and throwing it on the counter.

"You're welcome," I answered. My back and neck were killing me from all the computer work I'd done that day. "I think I'm going to head upstairs and take a hot bath and check out early," I said.

Donna nodded. "Sounds like a plan. I think I'll do the same."

I gave her a hug and headed upstairs to my room. I filled yet another fantastic tub, wondering who picked out Conner's bathroom fittings. Every bath in the house seemed to have a huge jetted tub. Once I had filled the tub with water and added lavender scented bath oil, I stripped down, twisted my hair up and secured it with a clip, and slid into the hot water.

Finally, after waiting an entire day for Lex to show up to continue our 'conversation', I felt like I could relax. It was almost ten and he wasn't back yet. I doubted we would have our talk tonight.

When the water began to cool, I climbed out of the tub and dried off. I wrapped the towel around me. It was a bit chilly in my room at night and I'd forgotten to bring my pajamas into the bathroom. I stepped into my bedroom and stopped short.

Lounging on my bed in all black, his shirt unbuttoned to reveal his toned chest and abs, was Lex. He was studying a sheaf of papers in his hand, his legs stretched out in front of him and crossed at the ankle. I realized his feet were bare. He looked completely relaxed and at home. His eyes lifted from the page to look at me, then his entire body went still.

"What are you doing in here?" I asked, tugging at my towel to be sure it covered me. Thank God, Conner and Donna had enormous bath sheets in their guest rooms. I moved to the dresser and grabbed the first nightshirt and shorts I could grab, snagging a pair of underwear at the same time. "Never mind. I don't care. I'm going to go into the bathroom and get dressed. Please be gone when I come out. If you want to talk to me, you can knock on the door like a normal person."

With that, I sailed into the bathroom and shut the door behind me. My hands were unsteady as I dressed. I never hesitated to speak like that with my other boyfriends, but Lex was different. You didn't tell Lex what to do. You asked him and hoped he would concede.

Sure enough, when I opened the door, Lex hadn't moved an inch. Somehow I knew that was his way of telling me that he was in charge. I leaned a shoulder against the door jamb between the bedroom and bathroom and crossed my arms over my chest.

Lex calmly continued to go through his paperwork, not looking at me. "Come here, Ivie."

I didn't move. I wanted to acquiesce, even felt my feet wanting to move without my direction, but I couldn't. I reminded myself that I had decided to keep my distance, that I was just food to this man unless I allowed him to change me in the most fundamental way.

Finally, he looked up from his paperwork, his dark eyes sharp. "Come here."

I shook my head.

He turned and put the papers on the nightstand next to him. Then he turned back and was studying my face intently. "What are you thinking?" he asked.

I didn't answer, glad that I seemed to have mastered the ability to hide my thoughts.

"Whatever it is, stop. I can promise that it is not that bad," he said gently. Lex lifted a hand to beckon me again.

"Lex, I can't do this." My voice was soft but firm.

"Do what?" His question seemed genuine, as if he sincerely wanted to know what I was thinking. That's the only reason I answered him.

"I can't get involved with you."

He cocked his head. "Why?"

"Lex, you left for two months without even saying good-bye. Then you show up and expect to pick up where we left off? Can you understand why I might be hesitant?"

He nodded, his face thoughtful.

Since he was listening, not arguing or brushing off my opinions, I decided to continue.

"There's another issue. I don't know about you, Lex, but I don't see my food source as equal. I wouldn't speak to a cow or chicken or treat them like I would another human being. While I would never be cruel to an animal, they are food and their existence ends in order to help me continue mine. I don't want to be the cow or chicken."

As I spoke, his eyebrows rose. When I finished, he no longer looked surprised. Instead he was scowling. I had to admit it was intimidating as hell.

He snapped his fingers. "Come here now."

I gave him wide eyes. "Excuse me?" He had not just snapped his fingers at me.

He growled. "You will not like it if I have to come to you."

With a sigh, I straightened from the door frame and walked to the bed. I stood at the end, arms hugging my midriff loosely.

"Sit down, Ivie. I won't bite."

I raised an eyebrow at him. His words were poorly chosen and almost funny. He didn't even react. I moved so that I was kneeling on the farthest corner of the bed from Lex. I sat back on my calves, keeping my eyes on him.

He didn't look pleased with my choice to sit as far away from him as possible, but he didn't say anything. Instead, he raised a knee and rested an arm on it, looking completely relaxed. Only the brightening of his dark brown eyes clued me in to the fact that he was disturbed. It was even more disconcerting to have him staring at me with those glowing eyes, as though he could see into my soul.

"I can see that you don't fully understand the relationship be-tween a vampire and their blood servant."

I clamped my jaw tight at his words. As he usually did, Lex saw the changes in my expression and body language and raised a hand.

"Please don't misunderstand. It's a literal translation. Basically, a blood servant is someone who serves blood. Not a servant, not property, not a slave. A better term would be gifter of blood, because we see the relationship as a gift. If a human shares their blood with us willingly and repeatedly, most of us value that beyond any other treasure. It is acceptance, something we rarely experience from most humans." He paused and saw that I was actively listening, so he continued. "You compare how you treat a cow or chicken with how I would treat you if you chose to share your blood with me. That's inaccurate and unfair. You haven't spent enough time around me, or vampires for that matter, to make that assumption."

There was a chiding undertone to his words and I couldn't help but feel a bit ashamed. Still, my previous experiences had been traumatic. How else would he expect me to view vampires?

"Well, I'm sorry you feel that way, Lex, but the first time I interacted with a vampire, he told me he intended to keep me as a pet. Not even a well-treated pet. In fact, I believe his exact words were, 'I'll keep you collared and leashed to the end of my bed and fuck your face, pussy, and ass at least once a night. If you behave and make sure I enjoy it, perhaps I'll even feed you and let you bathe.' I'm sure you'll understand if I am more than a bit hesitant to be involved with another of your kind."

The expression on Lex's face was thunderous. In fact, it was incredibly frightening. I started to inch back to the edge of the bed. I wasn't sure what he was thinking, but I was certain he was angry. When he saw my subtle retreat, his face cleared. His deep brown eyes were bright, almost the color of golden topaz, and the light emanating from them was so intense I could swear that it was burning my skin.

"I'm sorry to frighten you, little one. I did not know about his threats." He drew in a deep breath and the glow from his eyes lessened slightly. "Please come here. Please."

It was his pleading look and the gentle way he spoke to me that convinced me. I crawled forward a bit before Lex sat up, grasped my wrist, and tugged me against his long, hard body. He used his hand to push my head against his shoulder before he wrapped the same arm around me, pulling me flush to his side.

At first, I held my body rigidly, but he began to run his fingers through my hair and down my back, his strokes long and slow.

"You know that the vampire that attacked you is dead?" he asked.

I nodded, my cheek against his shoulder. The warm, light scent of his cologne filled my nostrils and I relaxed further into him. Before I realized what I was doing, I placed my hand on his chest, right between the open edges of his black shirt.

He squeezed me a bit tighter. "If I had known what he planned for you..." he trailed off.

I felt the steady beat of his heart beneath my palm. "What?" I asked.

"I would have made him suffer for weeks before I cut off his head."

His voice was so cold and furious that I shivered, even surrounded by his warmth.

"You killed him?" My voice was soft.

Lex's fingers stilled in my hair. "Yes. He committed treason. Once the Council found him guilty, he was put to death. Before I carried out his sentence, the Council charged me with interrogating him, using whatever means I deemed necessary. It's something I excel at and I could have kept him alive and in pain for a very long time."

My blood ran cold. I'd never understood that expression until that moment. Hearing the complete sincerity in Lex's voice, I knew that the vampire who kidnapped me would have suffered a great deal before he died.

Lex resumed stroking my hair. Slowly, my heart rate returned to normal and my insides warmed. Though the cold detachment Lex just demonstrated terrified me, he had never been anything but gentle or bossy with me. While his domineering ways were annoying, I didn't think he would hurt me the way my kidnapper had threatened.

"While it pains me to say this," Lex said, "tonight's conversation was a bit much. I can see that bad memories have returned for you. There is more for us to discuss, but it's getting late and you need sleep, little one." He pressed his lips to my forehead. "Climb under the covers."

While I pulled back the blankets and arranged my pillow the way I wanted it, Lex went through the room, turning off the light in the bath and the overhead light. The lamp was the last light he extinguished. I heard the rustle of clothing, but honestly didn't care. He had been correct when he said that our conversation brought forth bad memories.

Moments later, I felt his large, muscled form slide in behind me. Lex rolled me so that my cheek rested against his bare shoulder and my body cuddled into his side, just as we had been lying before, only now he was practically naked. I could feel the elastic waistband of his briefs through my thin nightshirt. Other than those tiny pieces of fabric, he was naked and warm.

I decided I was too damn tired to care, snuggled closer, and sighed. A few moments later, I was asleep.

Chapter Eight

THE NIGHT AIR was cold against my bare legs. I looked down and saw that I was wearing my nightshirt and baggy shorts. How did I get outside? And why in the hell was it cold? It was September in Texas. Night temperatures rarely dropped below the mid-seventies during the last part of summer.

"There you are."

My head shot up at that voice. That voice I would never forget, as long as I lived. The voice that promised to keep me locked up, naked, and abuse me in ways I didn't want to imagine. The voice of the man that kidnapped me, the man Lex said he'd killed.

In horror, I watched as he emerged from the shadows beneath the trees about twenty feet away. My heart stopped beating for a moment before it began to pound, fast and hard, against my ribs. My body suddenly felt as though it were encased in ice.

His low, sinister chuckle felt as though it were crawling up my spine. "Run, rabbit, run," he whispered.

At his words, I whimpered and spun around, taking off around the side of the house. I knew he could move fast, faster than I could, so I chose to angle through the trees with the hope that they would slow him down.

I was wrong. It didn't slow him down, only me. Just a few steps past the tree line, my bare foot caught in a tree root and I went sprawling face-down. A cry flew from my lips. God, that hurt. I was pretty sure I had broken my ankle.

I tried to scramble to my feet, but rough hands closed on my arms. I started to shriek in terror, but one of the hands clapped over my face, muffling the sound.

"I have you, Ivie."

My head jerked as I heard Lex's soothing voice next to my ear. How did he get into my dream?

"You're having a nightmare, little one. Wake up. Come back to me." His hand over my mouth moved to stroke my hair. "You're safe. I will keep you safe."

My eyes popped open in the darkened bedroom that I immediately recognized. I was in Conner and Donna's huge house, in their guest room. I wasn't in their backyard running for my life from a psychotic vampire.

I felt Lex move and then the lamp came on, the dim glow still bright enough to make me squint. The light served to chase away the last of the sticky shadows of the dream that clung to my consciousness.

I sat up, leaning back against the pillows, and scrubbed my hands over my face. I hadn't had the nightmare for several weeks now. In fact, the last time had been the night Lex and I had spent on the porch swing. I knew why. All the talk about my kidnapper, whose name I still didn't know and didn't care to know, and the memories that surfaced after.

Lex sat up next to me, the blankets tangled around his hips. "Do you want a glass of water?" he asked.

I shook my head and threw the comforter back. "Give me a minute. I'll be right back."

I was grateful that Lex seemed to understand that I was in desperate need of a toilet. I used the facilities and washed my hands. I splashed cool water on my face to wash away the clammy feeling that the sweat of fear left on my skin.

When I re-emerged from the bathroom, Lex was still in the bed, waiting for me. I climbed back under the blankets, yawning.

"Better?" He pulled me close as soon as I settled onto the mattress.

I nodded.

"Do you want to talk about it?" he asked.

I shook my head. "Sleep," I muttered.

Lex chuckled softly. "Are you sure you're okay?"

My eyes were closing, but I opened one to stare at him. "I'm tired. I'm tired of giving those stupid dreams power over me. I'm also physically tired. I just want to go back to sleep."

With his warm body cradling mine, I didn't think I would have much trouble.

"I understand," he murmured.

The lamp clicked off and I turned, putting my back to Lex. As I hoped, he stretched his long body behind mine, curving around me from shoulders down to ankles. He shoved his bottom arm under my pillow so my head was resting on it, then his top arm wrapped tightly around my waist.

As soon as he settled, I drifted back to sleep. It wouldn't register to me until much later that I never would have been able to go back to sleep without him there. His very presence made me feel safe.

✧ ✧ ✧

THE NEXT MORNING, I awoke alone, with my face buried in Lex's pillow and both arms wrapped tightly around it. I knew it was the pillow Lex had used because it smelled like him. I rolled over onto my back and sighed heavily.

While there were parts of last night's conversation that I'm glad I knew, I still couldn't believe I let him sleep in my bed. At least he was gone this morning, I thought. I needed some time to think about everything that he had said and what I believed. I would definitely be speaking to Donna about what Lex had told me.

I started when my bathroom door popped open and watched as Lex and a good amount of steam came through the door. The sight of his broad shoulders and defined and bulky muscles of his arms was enough to cause me to pause. What really took the cake was the sight of a stray droplet of water trailing from his collarbone, down the thick slabs of his pectorals and over the ridges of his abdomen, disappearing behind the bath sheet wrapped around his waist.

Though I had just been glad of them the night before, I was now cursing the huge towels that Conner and Donna kept in their guest baths. I wouldn't have minded seeing Lex sauntering out of that bathroom wrapped in nothing but a brief towel.

The incredible sight of his almost-naked body was enough to tempt me to throw all caution to the wind. I also seemed to lose the ability to think about what I was going to say before I opened my mouth.

"I thought you left," I said.

The corner of Lex's mouth quirked up. "No, not yet."

"I'm glad," I responded. I then had to check the urge to smack myself in the forehead. What the hell? I didn't need to be encouraging him.

His smirk became a full smile as he walked to the closet. I watched in utter amazement as he opened the door to the closet and disappeared inside. I sat up so I could watch as he walked directly to the back of the huge walk-in and pulled open a hidden door. On the other side, I saw another closet, this one holding a few pieces of men's clothing. I realized that Lex had the room next to mine and there was a hidden door between our closets.

His back was still to me as he grabbed a pair of briefs from the built-in dresser that ran along one wall of his closet. Then he dropped his towel and leaned over to put them on. I squeaked and had to force my eyes away. Holy shit, his ass was amazing. Even better than I imagined and I had a fantastic imagination. The rest of him wasn't bad either. In fact, the image would be burned in my retinas for all eternity. From now until the day I died, I would see a naked Lex from the rear on the back of my closed eyelids.

I threw the blankets back from the bed and made a mad dash for the bathroom. I worried that the longer I stayed in close proximity to an almost naked Lex, the closer I would be to forgetting all about my concerns and tackling him to the ground.

I did my necessary business and washed my hands and face, brushed my teeth, and tried to run a wide-toothed comb through my hair. Feeling a little more awake, I peeked out of the bathroom. Lex was standing at the end of the bed, buttoning his shirt, wearing pants and socks. Unsure whether I was relieved or disappointed that he was now almost fully dressed, I emerged from the bathroom, running a hand through my hair.

Lex turned and looked at me with a smile. "Feel better?"

I blushed and nodded. He finished buttoning his shirt and sat on the bed to slip on his shoes. Lex came over to me, smiling slightly as he looked down at my face.

"Hi," I said lamely.

His smile widened. "Hi."

I lowered my eyes to his throat.

"Ivie?" he said.

I looked up, back into his beautiful brown eyes with their long, thick lashes.

"We need to finish our talk tonight." He lifted his hand to my hair and wound a curl around his finger. "I want you to understand what's happening. Not only among vampires but between us."

I blinked at him. "So you're going to tell me what's going on?"

He nodded.

"I'm not sure about the rest, Lex. I'm still not sure how anything could work between us."

Lex leaned down and pressed a light kiss to my lips. "I know and I understand why you're worried. I think that you will feel better once we talk. Will you give me another chance to talk to you?" he asked.

The sweet, short kiss is what did it. When Lex was forceful and dominating, it turned me on. When he was sweet, I melted.

"I'll try," I sighed.

He grinned, yanking on the curl that was wound around his finger. "That's all I can ask for." He released my hair and stepped away to grab his suit jacket.

I watched as he shrugged into the black jacket. I wasn't positive, but I had a sneaking suspicion that his suit was Armani. The cut was superb, as was the fabric. Beneath the jacket, he wore a black shirt, no tie. He looked like a cross between a hot billionaire in the romances I read and a mob boss, sleek, sophisticated, and dangerous.

I managed not to drool, but barely. As though he read my mind, Lex smiled again.

"I'll be back shortly after nine."

I wanted to ask where he was going, but bit my tongue. I still didn't know him that well, despite the fact that he'd slept in my bed with me the last two nights. Now that I wasn't thoroughly freaked out, I realized I did have questions. Like the whole 'calling' thing. I wanted to understand how that worked. How could I have called him and forced him to come to me? He was a vampire. He had the ability to control my thoughts. It didn't make sense to me.

I touched his arm. "I'll be waiting."

His eyes grew hot. Suddenly, his hand was in my hair, tugging firmly, tilting my head back. "I like the sound of that," he growled before his mouth covered mine for a short, explosive kiss.

When he released me, my lips tingled as though they'd been touched with a live wire.

"I'll be back later," he said.

"Have a good day," I whispered.

He kissed me one last time and left. I stood next to the unmade bed I shared with him the night before, touching my lips, and wondering what I had just gotten myself into.

Chapter Nine

MY ANXIETY ABOUT my future talk with Lex was unfounded. Mostly because he never came back that night. Or the next. Or the next. At first I was hurt. He pursued me. He acted as though he wanted me. Now he was gone. Again.

Donna knew something was up. The third day he was gone, she was waiting for me in the kitchen after I got up late and showered. Two cups of coffee were sitting on the counter. One look at her face and I knew we were going to talk and I wasn't going to enjoy it. I hesitated by the door and considered making a run for it.

"Don't do it, Ivie. If I have to chase you down, you'll be wearing this coffee rather than drinking it."

I sighed. Donna grabbed both cups and headed toward me.

"Let's drink this out on the veranda."

It wasn't a request, so I followed her down the hall and out the back door. The morning was cooler than usual, but the light breeze felt fantastic. Donna went to a cafe style table and sat. Dreading the coming conversation, I did the same.

"I know what's going on between you and Lex," she said.

"There isn't anything going on between us."

She gave me a look. The look said not to treat her like she was stupid.

I sighed again. "I thought there was, but I've realized over the last few days that it's for the best if I keep my distance from Lex."

Donna shook her head. "You don't understand, Ivie. He's doing something very important and he doesn't have much choice."

I stared at my coffee cup, noticing for the first time that Donna had added cream and sugar exactly how I liked it.

"That may be, but I can't get involved with someone who is comfortable shoving his way into my life and then disappearing a few days later for God knows how long." She started to interrupt me, but I held up a hand. "Let me finish. Donna, he may be curing cancer but I don't know that because *he didn't tell me*. He could have picked up a phone and called. Hell, I would have understood a text even if the situation was dire. But no-call, no-show will get you fired from almost every job there is and, in my book, that applies for potential boyfriends."

Donna winced slightly. "He didn't call or text?"

I shook my head.

"Email?" she asked hopefully.

I laughed a little. "No."

"These archaic men. They use email and cell phones constantly for work but never think to pick it up to call or text for personal reasons." Donna leaned forward. "Listen, Ivie, I talked to Conner about this."

"What?" My voice was louder than I intended. "Why in the hell would you talk to Conner about this?"

"Well, he didn't want to talk about it, but I sort of cornered him in the shower this morning." That was more than I wanted to know, but Donna continued. "He doesn't know you like I do and I know this is bugging you."

I wanted to argue. I really did, but she was right and wrong. It wasn't bugging me. Lex's leaving without a word hurt me. More than it should have. I'd barely even kissed him or touched him and he had me tied up in knots. I had a feeling that once we got down to business, he would have the power to eviscerate me.

"Anyway, Conner said that what happened between you two was your business, blah, blah, blah." I smirked at her words. "You have to understand, Ivie. All this stuff happening between vampires. It's big. I mean, life changing, *world as we know it ending* big."

I stared at her. "What do you mean?"

Donna shook her head. "I can't explain it all."

I was beginning to get extremely annoyed with that attitude.

She must have read it on my face because she said, "Don't get mad. I honestly don't know everything." She sighed. "Did Lex not tell you about any of this?"

I shook my head.

"Goddammit. Stubborn fucker."

At her outburst, I laughed and laid a hand over hers. "Listen to me, Dee. You knew I was unsure about starting anything with Lex. I think this proves that I was right to be." I squeezed her hand. "He had his shot. Well, two shots really, and he walked away both times. Honestly, I'm glad he did because if I had invested any more of myself it would have been bad."

Her eyes grew soft and her hand turned under mine and returned my squeeze. "I'm sorry, Ivie, but I think you're wrong. I think Lex is serious about you, but he also has to deal with some serious shit right now. Unfortunately, though he's several hundred years old, he's not any smarter than a modern man when it comes to a relationship with women." She released my hand and stood up. "But, that's a conversation between you and him."

I stared at her, unsure of what to say.

"Are you hungry?" Donna asked.

I nodded.

"Let's go get some breakfast before I head to work."

Feeling even more unsettled than before, I picked up my coffee cup and followed her back into the house.

✧   ✧   ✧

TWO DAYS LATER, it was after midnight and I was cuddled under the downy comforter in the guest room, reading yet another romance novel on my Kindle. The author's description of the hero made me think of Lex. Actually, everything seemed to make me think of Lex.

Finally after two hours of trying to read, I tossed my Kindle to the side. This was ridiculous. He confused the hell out of me, offered to explain, then disappeared. I shouldn't be so consumed with thoughts of him. Still, I couldn't escape the memory of his voice growling that he liked the idea that I would be waiting for him when he returned.

Unfortunately, if he returned now, the only thing I would be waiting to do would be to give him a piece of my mind. Or at least the cold shoulder. Donna had been correct when she said that vampires of his age were just as clueless as modern men. Hell, I was sure they were more clueless because the women of their time had been sweet and subservient. And, after watching the way Conner's female employees fawned over him, I was pretty sure that the human women they were around of this century were too blinded by their good looks to tell them to take a flying leap when they were acting like jerks.

Well, with the exception of Donna. That night after dinner she had told Conner to go fuck himself when he suggested they skip the wedding she was in the midst of planning. As her maid of honor, I was equally pleased and disturbed by the idea that the wedding would be cancelled. I was looking forward to the affair because she was so radiantly happy. I was also dreading it because of the dark cloud of uncertainty and danger that seemed to be hanging over us all. A wedding would present an opportunity to strike for Conner and Lex's enemies.

Conner had laughed at her diatribe against Scottish fossils who wanted to ruin all her fun because of a few threats by dickless, weasely vampires. Then he'd thrown her over his shoulder, smacked her ass, and nodded to me.

"Excuse us, Ivie. I need to teach this lass a lesson." Then he'd calmly strode out of the kitchen with a cursing and squirming Donna over his shoulder.

They had disappeared, I assumed to their room, and never returned. I finished cleaning up the leftovers from dinner and spent a restless evening alternating between watching television and reading in the den.

Around ten, I'd decided to try and get some sleep. I headed upstairs, slipped into my last clean pajamas, which consisted of a black satin camisole and shorts covered in tiny white polka dots and edged with red lace. I desperately needed to do laundry the next day. Otherwise, I'd have nothing to wear but a pair of skintight black yoga pants and the dress shirt Lex had left in my room before he left.

After tossing and turning for an hour, I decided to try and read a little more. With each page, I started to see Lex more and more clearly in the role of the hero in the book. Sick of it, I finally gave up and stared at the ceiling.

If it hadn't been so late, I would have texted Shannon or Ricki, but I knew they would both be asleep at this time of night. Maybe a stroll around the backyard would help relax me. I threw aside the covers and was about to slide my feet into a pair of flip flops when I heard the loud chiming of the doorbell.

At first I froze in fear, then shook my head. If someone meant us all harm, I doubt they would have rung the bell at the gate. I left my room and crept toward the staircase that led to the front of the house. I heard two male voices as I approached the railing at the top of the stairs. I peeked over and froze.

Conner stood at the door, shirtless, which was a sight striking enough to cause any girl to pause, but that wasn't what caused me to freeze. He was talking to a man dressed in a dark red shirt and a pair of dark jeans that clung to his body in all the right places. I realized that the guy was Finn, who I'd met at the engagement party. He had been kind and very flirty. He was also drop-dead gorgeous. I hadn't talked to him much because Lex had glowered at us during our short conversation and it made me antsy as hell.

While Lex was rough around the edges and radiated testosterone more than a perfect face, Finn was a work of art. His cheekbones were high and carved and his lips were sensuous, full without being effeminate. It was Finn's eyes that struck a chord with me though. They were such a deep blue that they appeared purple. And they were observant and wise. This was a man who saw and had seen everything. He learned from both his mistakes and those of others. Those eyes, combined with his fallen angel face and long chestnut hair, made it hard to look at him without having at least one wild fantasy about him dressed in furs, riding a huge steed into battle while wielding an ax.

Finn and Conner were speaking in low tones. Suddenly, Finn's purple eyes lifted to mine and they burned with intensity. I felt goose bumps rise along my arms and neck. The weight and power of his gaze was like nothing I'd ever felt. Then he smiled, breaking the trance that I had fallen into when I stared into his eyes.

"Ivie!" he called, his eyes wandering over my body. "I must say that is a very fetching outfit."

I rolled my eyes and tossed a few stray curls out of my face as I headed down the stairs. While the satin was thin, the pajamas covered me from upper chest to mid-thigh. The set didn't even show cleavage.

"Hi, Finn. How are you?" I asked.

He reached out and snagged my wrist, yanking me forward for a quick hug. His body was warm and hard and he smelled like the night, dark and mysterious. Of their own volition, my arms wrapped around his torso for a quick squeeze before I dropped them and tried to step back.

Finn's hands cupped my bare shoulders, intensifying the goose bumps on my flesh. While I didn't feel the electricity from his touch as I did Lex's, there was an undercurrent, a pulse of power, where each of his fingertips rested on bare skin. He lowered his head so his face was close to mine, but Conner spoke, causing him to pause.

"Finn," he said warningly. "Don't forget about Lex."

Finn's face stayed close to mine, his mouth only inches from my lips, but his eyes flicked over my shoulder to treat Conner with an intense stare.

"I don't see Lex anywhere near, do you?" he asked.

My tummy twisted painfully at his words. The reminder that Lex had found it easy to walk away from me wasn't pleasant. Finn's eyes returned to mine and he looked at me as though he were searching for something in my face.

"I'm sorry, Ivie," he said softly.

I shrugged. "I'm not sure what you're referring to."

One corner of his mouth kicked up. "I'm sure," he murmured.

His hands caressed the bare skin of my shoulders, causing me to shiver slightly, before he released me.

"Now, I'm sorry to ask this of you, but Conner and I need a few moments to speak. Could you excuse us?"

I nodded and glanced at Conner, forcing my eyes on his face. He might be a gorgeous hunk of man meat, but he was also my best friend's fiancé. It wouldn't be right to ogle him.

"How about I make some coffee?" I asked.

He smiled tightly at me. "Make it tea and that would be perfect."

Though Conner was Scottish, I rarely saw him drink tea. Still, I didn't even bat an eye at his request. I headed into the kitchen and filled the kettle on the stove. While I waited for the water to boil, I got down a teapot and filled it with hot water from the tap to warm it. Then I spooned loose tea into a large mesh tea ball. As the kettle began to whistle, I removed it from the heat before I poured the hot water out of the teapot into the sink.

Focusing on my task rather than the possible reasons for Finn's late night visit, I placed the tea ball in the pot and poured the hot water over it. After a few minutes of searching, I found a tray. I heard the kitchen door open behind me and glanced over my shoulder.

Donna was standing in the doorway, looking mussed and a little sleepy, but also worried.

"Here, let me help," she said.

She grabbed four cups, the sugar bowl, and poured some milk into a little pitcher. We placed it all on the tray. I let her carry it into the study because I didn't trust myself not to drop the entire thing on the floor.

When we entered the study, Conner was seated behind his desk, looking grim. Finn was sprawled on the sofa near the fireplace, one arm stretched along the back and his legs straight in front of him, crossed at the ankle. Donna placed the tray on the desk and started pouring tea. She added sugar and milk to one and handed it to me. I thanked her and decided to sit next to Finn on the couch. Mostly, because his appreciative eyes were making me a little uncomfortable and there was a blanket tossed over the back of the sofa.

As Donna poured the rest of the tea and gave Conner and Finn theirs, I put my cup down on the table next to the couch and grabbed the throw. I sat on the cushion, pulled my legs up to sit cross-legged, and draped the soft chenille around me. After I grabbed my cup and took a sip, I glanced around. Conner was contemplating his tea while Donna stood next to him, running a comforting hand over his shoulder. Finn was smiling slightly as he looked at me, as though he understood that he unsettled me and thought it was funny that I felt the need to cover up.

His astuteness and subsequent amusement made me feel a little foolish for rushing to wrap myself up like a mummy. Rather than show my embarrassment, I gave him a bland look and continued to drink my tea. His little smile widened into a shit-eating grin, but he said nothing.

Finally, Donna broke the silence. "Okay, I hate to interrupt this wonderful awkward moment we have going, but will someone please explain to me what's happening?" She looked at Finn. "I enjoy your company, Finn, but you typically don't show up here in the middle of the night without calling first."

Finn put his cup on the side table without taking a sip. "I have some news. Important news."

Donna and Conner both came to attention. I focused on keeping my hands steady as tension filled the room.

I watched Finn straighten, his face serious. "There is a new group forming among vampires. They're calling themselves The Faction."

I wanted to snort at the name because it lacked originality, but, somehow, I knew that would be a bad idea. I could sense that the men wouldn't appreciate an attempt at levity.

"And their goals?" Conner asked. His face was deadly serious.

Finn glanced at me before he continued. "They want vampires to reveal themselves and take control."

Before I could think better of it, I asked, "Take control of what?"

All eyes were on me and I felt a flush creep up my neck and chest.

"Everything," Finn replied.

Well, shit. I had a bad feeling that Donna's wedding was just cancelled, and that was going to be the least of our problems.

Chapter Ten

NONE OF US slept the rest of that night. I couldn't contribute to the discussion, but I was worried and frightened. I listened as Conner and Finn outlined the situation. Donna didn't have a lot to say either, though she did ask a lot of questions. Most of them were the same questions I had.

After Finn outlined what The Faction had planned, Conner asked, "Do you know who the members are?"

"I have nine names. One of them belongs to their leader."

Conner smiled, but it was cold and vicious and very, very scary. "Names?"

"Cornelius the Slayer is the leader."

I couldn't help it. I snorted a giggle. I tried to cover it with a cough, but, with the way the men were looking at me, I could tell I wasn't fooling anyone. What the fuck? Cornelius was the dorkiest name. And I was almost one hundred percent certain he called himself 'The Slayer' to sound more menacing. Like a pimply-faced, high school geek who played Diablo, or whatever that damn online role-playing game was called.

At least Donna understood why I was struggling with mirth. I glanced at her and bugged out my eyes and she suddenly developed the same cough I had before. Finn shifted on the sofa next to me, bringing my eyes to him. He was staring at me as if I'd grown an extra head, though an underlying hint of amusement glimmered in his eyes.

Conner gave Donna an exasperated smile, as though he couldn't decide if he wanted to kiss her, spank her, or both. Even though that smile wasn't intended for me, I couldn't stop the little flutter in my belly at the thought of any man looking at me like that. A sliver of jealousy pierced my heart. I wanted that for myself and I wanted it badly.

"I'm sorry," I sucked in a deep breath. "It's just, Cornelius *the Slayer*?" I squeaked.

At my words, Donna dissolved into giggles, unable to hide them behind a cough any longer. It took me several seconds to get myself under control as well. When the two of us calmed down, both Conner and Finn were staring at us, their expressions stony.

"I don't understand what in the hell is funny about a vampire who has earned the name *Slayer* because of the thousands of humans, vampires, and other supernatural beings he has slaughtered," Conner stated softly.

Donna and I instantly stopped laughing. Conner was right. That wasn't funny at all.

"I'm sorry," I whispered.

I felt a hand on my knee and looked down to see Finn's fingers squeeze my leg gently before he released me. I stared at my leg, wondering if his hand left marks because every place his hand had touched was tingling. God, I was turning into vamp tramp!

"It's all right, Ivie." Finn's voice distracted me from my contemplation of my leg.

Still, I felt like a heel for giggling about this guy. It was obvious that, even if Donna and I thought his name was stupid, his intentions were serious and, likely, deadly.

Finn turned back to Conner. "I will give you a list of the other eight names, but there is something else." He paused and I could tell he was searching for the right words. "There are more members, all secret, and The Faction is still recruiting. The Council and the investigators still don't know how many vampires are truly involved."

That didn't sound promising, I thought.

Conner's brows lowered and he tapped his lip as he thought. "It may give us an opportunity to plant a spy within the group. You and I need to approach the Council with a list of appropriate candidates."

Finn nodded before he turned to Donna and then me. "Ladies, I don't want to exclude you from the conversation, but there are things I must discuss with Conner that must, by vampire law, stay between Council members."

Donna nodded, clearly used to this sort of thing. I wanted to argue and ask a million questions, but the usual good-humored sparkle in Finn's eyes was long gone. I knew with one glance at his expression, that I did not want to piss him off right now.

So, Donna and I went into the kitchen to make a pot of strong coffee and put together a light breakfast. I watched her move around the kitchen, her face pale and pinched.

"Are you okay?" I asked.

"Yes. Just tired."

It hit me that Donna had been trapped in this house with me for a while now. I wondered if she had been drinking as much blood as she should. While I didn't want to contemplate my best friend sucking the life out of someone, I also didn't want her to get sick or hurt. I had already been through that nightmare.

"Do you need blood?" I asked quietly.

She blinked at me, her eyes huge. "What?"

I took a step toward her. "You haven't left the house. You're paler than usual. Do you need blood?" I swallowed hard, unable to believe I was about to say what I intended to say next. "If you need it, tell me. I, uh, I will give you blood."

She stared at me, her eyes huge. "Are you offering to give me your blood, Ivie?" she asked slowly.

Even though the thought terrified me, I was. I wanted my friend to be safe and healthy. I nodded.

Suddenly, Donna grinned hugely. "Wow. I think that's the nicest thing you've ever done for me, especially considering how you feel about being a snack for a vamp." She laughed a little. "Don't worry. Conner and I shared blood last night before we went to bed. We get most of our sustenance from each other."

I wrinkled my nose. I was no expert on vampires, but I always assumed they needed human blood to survive.

Donna saw my expression. "It's complicated," she sighed. "I'll have to explain it to you later. It will take a while."

I nodded and busied myself washing the cups and teapot from our middle of the night tea. Honestly, I wasn't sure I wanted to know. Donna's voice stopped me.

"Seriously, Ivie. Thank you for offering. It means a lot to me." She paused, her eyes far away. "I know you've had a lot of trouble adjusting to the changes over the last few months."

I smiled at her. "I would do whatever it took to keep you safe and healthy, Dee. You know that."

She nodded, her eyes filling with tears.

"And, for God's sake, don't cry or I'll be bawling too!" I exclaimed, continuing to wash the dishes.

She blinked rapidly. "I was just so afraid that, after what happened..." she trailed off.

I removed my hands from the dishwater and dried them before I walked over to her and hugged her close. Her arms wrapped around me, squeezing me tightly.

"I love you," she whispered.

My own throat felt tight so my voice was barely audible as well. "I love you too."

She released me and cleared her throat. "Okay, enough mushy shit."

I laughed and went back to washing the dishes while she finished brewing the coffee. After the coffee and food were done, Donna went in search of the men. We all sat down and ate together. Conner and Finn were obviously concerned, but they made an effort to carry on a conversation and create a sense of normalcy.

They excused themselves once the food was gone and Donna and I began to clean up. I still couldn't believe that vampires could eat. It went against all the stories and myths I'd heard.

"Well, I'm going upstairs to get ready for work," Donna said after the last clean dish was put away.

I looked at her in surprise. "Conner is letting you go into work today?"

She snickered. "As if he can tell me what to do. Yes, I'm going to work. Though, I have to take two of his men with me for personal security."

She had a point. Nobody bossed Donna around. Not even uber-alpha Conner. Well, sometimes she let him get away with it, the rest of the time I often thought she was doing her best to give him the world's worst migraine.

I followed her up the stairs. "I'm going to clean up and try to work as well, I guess. If I don't try to do something, I'm just going to sit around and brood."

Donna stopped just outside the guest room door with me. "I'm really sorry about the situation with Lex, Ivie. I still think that he's serious about you. I just don't think he's used to having to answer to someone else."

I shrugged. "That may be, but I've had doubts even before he went out of his way to convince me to give him a shot. I think it's best if I forget about Alexander Dimitriades."

Donna stared at me, her expression unreadable. After a few seconds, she sucked air into her nose loudly. "Fine. I still think you're making a mistake, but you have to do what you think is best."

I grinned. Donna would always support me, even if she thought I was being an idiot. Though, she didn't hesitate to tell me so.

"Thanks, Dee. I'll see you tonight, okay?"

"Yeah, yeah. Just tell me to get lost."

We both laughed and I went into my room and showered. I dressed in my only clean clothes, a pair of black yoga pants and a deep purple shirt I found in the bottom of my suitcase. I really had to do some damn laundry. It was one of the few non-black clothing items I owned. I bought it because the color made my pale skin glow and my brown eyes pop. I even put on a little make-up.

While I wasn't necessarily interested in attracting a vampire, I still didn't want to look like dogshit while tons of attractive men were in the house. After I tamed my curls, I grabbed my laptop and headed downstairs to the den. I stopped by the kitchen for a bottle of water before I walked down the hall to the comfortably appointed room. I settled on a couch and opened my computer. I set it on the coffee table while it booted up, stretching my arms above my head. I would do a couple of hours of work and then think about taking a nap.

Then, while I waited for the computer to finish booting up, I leaned my head back as I released a jaw-cracking yawn and promptly fell into a deep, dreamless sleep.

✧   ✧   ✧

"Ivie."

I turned my head away from that voice. I was comfy, warm, and tired. I planned to sleep for the next two weeks.

"Ivie, sweet one, it's time to wake up."

I grunted and batted away the hand that was pushing my hair back from my face. "Go away if you want to live," I growled.

The sudden silence at my words was followed by loud, deep laughter. When I realized who was sitting with his hip pressed into my side, my eyes popped open and I sat straight up on the couch, my hair flying everywhere.

"Jesus, Finn, if you want to kill me, just use a gun next time," I gasped, pressing a hand to my pounding heart.

He was still chuckling as he watched me try to regain my composure. "Of course. Though I doubt you'll be of use to me dead."

There was a flirtatious gleam in his eye that made my tummy flutter. I sighed and shoved a mass of my curly hair out of my face. I just hoped it wasn't sticking out around me like a lampshade.

"So, what's going on?" I asked.

"It's time for dinner. Donna asked me to come wake you."

I blinked in shock. I had been asleep for the entire day?

"Um, okay. I'll be right there. I just need a second to wake up."

He nodded and rose gracefully, striding to the door with a rolling gait that made me appreciate the way his jeans fit. When I was sure he was gone, I blew out a deep breath. What in the hell was it with me and vampires?

I got up and went to the powder room before I headed into the kitchen. The meal was delicious and the company entertaining. Finn and Conner weren't as serious as they had been that morning. In fact, Finn insisted on telling stories of his times with Conner in Europe while Conner was still a baby vamp. Donna and I laughed loud and often.

After we were done eating, Donna and Conner insisted on washing up, so Finn and I went out on the veranda. He went directly to the porch swing. The very same one I had sat on with Lex. I started to move for a chair just to the side of the swing, but Finn patted the seat.

"Come sit with me."

I couldn't refuse without looking like a complete ass, so I walked over and settled on the swing next to him. Just like Lex, he rested his arm across the back of the swing. One major difference was that Finn gave me my space. He didn't press so close that I could practically feel the imprint of his ribs against mine. Still, I was tense.

"Relax, Ivie," he said. His voice was deeper, more mellow, than I'd ever heard it before. It wound around me like a warm blanket and made my tense muscles turn to jelly. Holy hell, a voice like that was a lethal weapon.

I found myself leaning back into the swing, bringing my shoulders in contact with his arm as he used his foot to push the swing. All the while, his fingers ran through my hair, wrapping strands around his fingers before releasing them. It felt heavenly.

"Have you heard from Lex?" he asked quietly, his black magic voice may have been soothing, but his question was not.

I sat up straighter. "No." I didn't say anything else.

"Not interested, sweet one?"

I shot him a sidelong glance that made him smile. "I don't think that's any of your business," I answered primly.

His fingers, which had been so soothing just moments before, tightened in my hair, forcing me to turn my head so he could look directly into my eyes. I gasped when I saw that his irises were glowing like amethysts in the moonlight. It was a beautifully haunting sight, those gem-like eyes set in the face of an angel.

"I plan to make it my business if the answer is what I want it to be."

I felt a small streak of heat pierce my abdomen. While it felt incredibly nice, it was nothing like the insane sensations that Lex inspired within me.

I bit my lower lip. Finn's eyes tracked the motion. I realized that I now understood how a mouse felt when it faced a large, hungry cat. What was it about these damn vampires?

Then the light in his eyes dimmed and he blinked. "I can see the answer isn't the one I wanted."

I opened my mouth, then shut it with a snap. I wasn't about to argue with him about this. If I told him Lex didn't matter, I had a feeling he'd be on me like Garfield on lasagna, gobbling me up in huge bites. While the thought wasn't completely unattractive, it was intense and more than a little scary.

Finn's mouth quirked as though he could hear my internal monologue. Considering I was still mastering the skill of shielding my thoughts, he may very well have heard every single one. Still, he didn't say a word of it. Instead, he used my hair to pull my face even closer to his.

"Okay, sweet one. I can see that you are conflicted. I know you want to tell me you aren't interested, but your body says different-ly."

Again, I started to open my mouth to argue only to shut it quickly. The damn vampire had a point. Every time he touched me, my heart sped up slightly and my skin tingled. I couldn't help it. That didn't mean I wanted to pursue anything with him.

"So, I'll give you time," he announced with a wicked grin. "Though I can't promise not to do everything in my power for the next few weeks to change your mind."

I shivered, which caused him to chuckle. With the deeper tones, his laugh was like a hand drifting down my spine, warm, slow, and sexy.

He leaned forward and placed his lips lightly on mine. The kiss was gentle and sweet, though he ended it with a quick nip of my bottom lip that made me gasp.

"Go on inside, Ivie. I'm going to sit in the dark and think of how much I like the way you taste."

My bottom lip throbbed as I jumped off the swing and scurried in the house. I avoided the kitchen, where I could hear Ivie and Conner bickering good-naturedly, and headed straight up to my room. Once I reached the safety of the guest room, I darted inside and shut the door behind me. It seemed I was constantly seeking the safety of my room while I stayed with Donna.

Finn was a walking contradiction, hell, even that damn kiss was a contradiction. One second it was soft, light, and undemanding, then he ended it with a slight sting. And what he had said to me when he told me to go inside. I should be a puddle at his feet.

What upset me the most, though, was the knowledge that I would have given him whatever he wanted if only he had been Lex.

Chapter Eleven

OVER THE NEXT WEEK, I couldn't escape Finn. He appeared at Conner's house every day. Sometimes, he would give me a smile and nod on his way in or out and other times he would stay for dinner and chat with everyone. Then, after Conner and Donna would go to bed, he and I would hang out together, talking, playing cards, or even watching movies.

After six days of this, I finally had to say something. He and I were sitting in the library, playing Scrabble and drinking wine. As he was wiping the floor with me at the word game, he told me stories about his life. If I hadn't known how long he'd lived, I never would have believed half of them. Still, I supposed that almost a thousand years of existence would present a person with opportunities to make all kinds of hilarious and sometimes dangerous choices.

As I giggled at a particularly funny story he told me about an eighteenth century bordello he visited 'once or twice', I noticed that he stared at me intently. Not just me, but my mouth in particular. My smile died and I took a nervous sip of my wine, but his eyes stayed glued to my lips.

Suddenly, he was no longer in the chair across from me, but crouched beside my seat, his face almost level with mine. I hadn't seen him move. Taken off guard, I squeaked and cringed back in the seat, but a firm, hot hand cupped my neck, preventing me from escaping. Despite the scare he gave me, I felt my blood heat at his touch.

Finn leaned forward and brushed his lips against mine. He pulled back just enough so that all I could see were his deep purple eyes.

"You taste much better than the wine," he murmured.

Then he tried to devour me. His kiss was ruthless, teeth nipping and tongue thrusting into my mouth. Though I felt my body respond, I knew deep within me that this was wrong. I didn't belong with Finn. The vampire I really wanted had left me for the second time and still hadn't contacted me almost two weeks later.

I placed a hand against Finn's chest and pushed lightly. I knew that trying to force him to back away wouldn't work. He pulled away slightly, his lips red from the kiss and his eyes glowing like two jewels.

Unable to stop them, I felt tears fill my eyes and one trickle down my cheek. "I'm sorry," I whispered. "I can't. It doesn't feel..." I searched for my next word carefully but came up woefully empty, "right."

It was lame in terms of an explanation, but it was all I could offer, because it truly didn't feel right. As much as I enjoyed Finn's company and liked him, he wasn't Lex. Just as I had in the past, I wanted what I couldn't have. A pony when I was five, the prom king when I was sixteen, a size four ass at twenty-one, and, now, Alexander Dimitriades.

Finn's thumb swiped under my eye, catching the single tear. "Don't be sorry, sweet one. If your heart belongs to another, it isn't yours to give any longer."

My eyes widened, tears forgotten. "But my heart doesn't belong to anyone," I denied.

His expression was beautiful as he studied my face. Beautiful and sad. "Doesn't it?" he asked.

I shoved the chair back and stood, pacing around the table where we had been sitting. I yanked at the ends of my hair, anxious for something to do with my hands.

"I don't know. I can't stop thinking about him."

Finn stood and walked over to the window, looking out at the moonlit night. "Lex?" he asked absently.

I nodded then realized he wasn't looking at me. "Yes," I answered.

He turned to me, his eyes piercing. "Do you know how Lex feels about you?" he asked.

I shook my head. "I haven't heard from him in almost two weeks."

Finn chuckled, but it wasn't a happy sound, and ran a hand over his face and through his long brown hair. "Foolish Greek. He's old enough to know better."

I looked at him in confusion and then Finn's smile became sincere.

"Well, if I cannot take you for a lover, I would be pleased to have you as a friend."

Cautiously, I nodded, my heart still pounding and head still buzzing from the feelings his kiss evoked, as well as my own confusion and frustration over Lex.

Calmly, Finn sat back down at the table and picked up his wine glass. "Should we continue our game?"

Unable to think of a reason why we shouldn't, I shrugged and sat down across from him and promptly lost.

That night had been two days ago. Finn still made an effort to talk to me, making me laugh often, and sometimes he flirted shamelessly. It was Friday night and we were both sprawled on

Conner's huge sofa in his home theater, watching movies. Conner and Donna were at a business dinner and Finn had come round at Conner's behest. With such spotty knowledge of The Faction, they were not going to let me stay home alone, even though I argued that I would be safe with Conner's top-notch security system and panic room, well, apartment, in his basement.

So, as punishment, I forced Finn to watch a sappy romantic comedy with me. Surprisingly, he watched the movie without complaint. We munched on popcorn and I drank a diet soda with rum. He sipped a beer. It felt like hanging out with any one of the guy friends I'd had in college. It was kind of nice.

As the ending credits rolled, Finn looked over to me, wrapping one of my curls around his finger. I wasn't sure what it was with these damn vampires and my curly hair, but they seemed to enjoy touching it.

"So are all the men of this age such pussies?" he asked.

I choked on my drink. "What?"

"Well, the man in that movie basically allowed her to lead him around by his dick," he commented.

I rolled my eyes. Apparently, men hadn't changed in the past thousand years or so, because I'd heard this particular complaint after a chick flick before. It seemed that the Y chromosome made men incapable of understanding why any man would want to bend over backwards for a woman.

As he toyed with my hair, Finn said, "Though, for an arse like hers, I might be willing to put up with that for a bit myself."

I couldn't help it. It was such a *guy* thing to say. I broke down into giggles. For some reason, I found his macho attitude hilarious. Probably because he looked like a fairy-tale prince, yet sounded just like a modern guy.

I rested my forehead against his shoulder as I laughed, my eyes watering.

"What the fuck is going on here?"

I jumped as a deep voice bellowed just before the lights came on. I squinted against the brightness. Finn and I had been sitting in the darkened theater to watch the movie. I looked toward the door to see Lex framed in the doorway, dressed all in black and looking furious. Well, more than furious.

Finn smiled lazily. "Good evening, Alexander. I didn't realize you were on your way back."

He slowly unwound my hair from his finger, but still rested his arm along the back of the sofa. Lex watched the movement closely, his eyes burning with dark fire. Then his gaze zeroed in on my face.

I shivered. Holy shit, he was enraged. For the first time, I worried that Lex might actually hurt me.

"Ivie and I were discussing the film we just watched."

Lex's eyes snapped back to Finn's face and scrutinized him closely. Then he looked back at me.

Lifting a hand, palm up, he said, "Ivie, come here."

I sucked in a shaky breath. For reasons I didn't want to examine, I wanted to do as he asked. Every time he spoke to me in that tone, I wanted to melt in a puddle at his feet and do whatever he wanted. At that moment, however, I wasn't sure he wouldn't rip me to shred when I came within reach.

He must have seen the true fear in my expression because he closed his eyes and dropped his head. I saw him inhale deeply several times before he lifted his head again. His eyes were less intense and he no longer appeared murderous.

"I would never hurt you, little one, not in a way you would not enjoy. Come to me."

Somehow, I knew he was talking about hurting me in a sexual way. In a way that made my tummy flutter and my pulse thrum. Still unsure, I glanced at Finn. I thought I heard Lex growl, but I wasn't sure. It was Finn's small nod that convinced me I would be safe with Lex.

Slowly, I got to my feet and walked toward the huge, angry vampire standing statue still in the doorway. When I got within reach, he lunged forward and I gasped. Before I knew what was happening, he threw me over his shoulder in a fireman's hold.

"Lex, put me down," I said quietly.

"Fuck no," was his terse reply.

"Please, Lex," I said.

Whatever I had been planning to say flew right out of my head as his palm connected sharply with the cheek of my ass.

After that, I knew it would be useless to try and argue, so I let him carry me out of the house and straight to his large, black SUV. Without a word, he dumped me in the backseat, his face taut with suppressed rage.

"Seatbelt," he snapped.

My hands shaking, I sat up and buckled myself into the seat. I watched as Lex climbed in behind the steering wheel.

"Lex," I whispered.

"Don't speak."

His voice cracked through the interior of the car like a whip. I saw the muscle in the side of his jaw working. I had a bad feeling that my perception of things between us was not the same as his. In fact, I was getting the impression that I misunderstood the entire situation. Just as Donna had suggested. Why didn't I ever learn to listen? This wasn't the first time she'd been right and I'd ignored her advice.

I huddled in the back of the car, trying to control the tremors in my limbs. I recognized the route we were taking. Lex was incredibly pissed and he was taking me home. To his home.

We arrived before I was ready. I reached down to open the passenger door, but the child lock was engaged. I peeked over the top of the front seat and saw that Lex had both hands on the steering wheel, gripping it so tightly I thought it was going to snap in half.

"Ivie, I'm going to offer you one chance to escape. If you really don't want this, want me, tell me now. If you can tell me that sincerely, I'll take you back to Conner's and never bother you again. If you can't, then you're mine to do with as I please."

My stomach twisted viciously with fear and arousal. Considering how angry he was, I wanted to beg him to take me back to the safety of Donna's McMansion. But I wanted Lex more. For the last two weeks, I'd been unable to get the thought of him out of my mind.

"I'll stay," I whispered.

I watched as he bowed his head and flexed his fingers. After a moment, he unbuckled his seatbelt and got out of the car. I was struggling with the clasp on my belt when my door opened and he hauled me out. His fingers manacled my wrist so tightly I was fairly certain I'd have marks. I didn't care.

His dark eyes looked black and surprisingly cold when he stared down at me. "Tonight, you do not speak unless I ask you a direct question. And when you answer, you do so out loud and you call me Sir. Do you understand?"

I shuddered and nodded. His hand whipped up and tangled in my hair, tugging my head back roughly. It was on the edge of being too painful, but never crossed the line.

"How do you answer?" he demanded.

Crap, I'd already forgotten. I had to say it aloud. "Y-y-yes, Sir," I stammered.

He nodded, his grip on my hair relaxing slightly. His gaze moved over my face, detached but keen. "If you need me to stop, all you have to say is zebra. I can promise that I'll stop what I'm doing immediately. Do you understand?" he asked.

"Yes, Sir." My voice was a bit stronger this time.

"What will you say if you need to stop?"

"Zebra, Sir."

He nodded, his face relaxing even more. My heart was pounding in my chest like a bass drum, hard and fast. Dear God, this insane feeling careening around inside me was what I imagined when I'd asked my previous boyfriend to dominate me, only it hadn't worked like that before.

His hand in my hair became a caress. "Even if I stop tonight, Ivie, I won't let you leave. You chose to stay and you will stay until I am done with you."

At his possessive words and the dark fire in his eyes, so at odds with the now-gentle movements of his hand in my hair, I began to pant. Every cell in my body was on high alert and a mixture of anticipation and fear twined within my belly.

Then Lex smiled and it was wicked. And just for a moment, I wondered if I had just sold my soul to the Devil.

Chapter Twelve

WITHOUT ANOTHER WORD, he turned and started toward the house. I almost tripped going up the short flight of stairs that led to Lex's front door. My knees were weak and my thighs felt like overcooked noodles. Lex unlocked the front door and pulled me inside, his hand still tight around my wrist.

He moved me deliberately, positioning me next to him as he locked the front door. My breaths were light and shallow. He still didn't speak as he led me through the house to a plain black door. When I saw it, I realized exactly how serious Lex was about his kink.

I didn't have time to decide if that terrified me or not, because he opened the door to reveal a flight of stairs descending to a lower level. Lex didn't even spare me a glance, merely started down the steps as though he expected me to follow, which I did because he still had my wrist in his grip.

It was dark but Lex hit a few switches along the wall and lights came on throughout the room. He had recessed lighting through-out the space, and each fixture pointed to specific play areas of his dungeon. And it was definitely a dungeon. Though I'd never seen one except in my imagination or on the videos I sometimes watched online, I was sure this was a place for torture and pleasure.

Beneath one pool of light was a St. Andrew's Cross. What looked like a spanking bench sat beneath another. There were pieces of furniture I didn't recognize and wasn't sure I wanted to know what they were intended for. A huge bed, large enough for five or six people, stood in the center of the room, the wooden headboard carved to look like twisted, thorny vines and I assumed the style made it easier to secure someone to the bed. A huge black cabinet stood against the wall to my left, the doors shut tight. Floggers, restraints, paddles, and other paraphernalia hung along the same wall.

My heart was definitely about to pound its way out of my chest. Lex was serious about his play and I was a novice. The tension inside me ratcheted up another ten notches. I wasn't sure I could handle whatever he planned to dish out.

I didn't realize that I was no longer breathing until both of Lex's hands cupped my jaw and tilted my head up so he could look into my eyes. Whatever he saw there, or felt emanating from me, made the anger drain from his expression. Concern replaced the rage.

"Breathe, little one," he prompted.

I managed to suck a deep breath in past the tightness in my throat.

"Another."

I exhaled and sucked in another breath until the urge to throw up, pass out, or both, lessened.

His thumbs moved in circles on the hinge of my jawbone. "Ivie, I'm sorry I scared you. I promise, you are safe with me."

I blew out that breath and forced myself to take another.

"I know," I whispered. "I just got a little overwhelmed when you brought me down here." I gestured around us. "I knew you were into kink but I wasn't exactly expecting something this, um…." I trailed off, unable to think of how to describe what I saw around me.

His dark chocolate eyes brightened for a moment. "I can see how that might take you off guard." He grew serious. "Do you want to go back upstairs?" he asked quietly. "I don't want you to feel as though this is something you have to do tonight."

My mouth went completely bone dry. Even though he was seriously pissed off and, judging from the tent in the front of his pants, even more turned on, this powerful vampire was willing to take my thoughts and feelings into consideration. That alone convinced me I had made the correct choice.

"No, I don't want to go back upstairs," I said, my voice a little stronger than before.

Lex's eyes bored into mine for what felt like an eternity. I wondered if he was reading my mind. Or perhaps he was struggling with himself. Finally, he seemed to be satisfied with what he saw and his hands released my jaw.

"Very well," he said. He gestured to a small pillow nearby. It sat beneath another recessed fixture, looking as though it were under a spotlight. "Remove your shirt and pants and kneel on that."

I gulped and walked to the cushion. I pulled my shirt over my head, folding it neatly, trying to stall without being obvious. I set it on the floor next to the pillow. Then I stripped off my yoga pants, also folding them neatly and placing them on top of the shirt. I didn't remove my bra or panties. He hadn't said anything about them and I honestly felt vulnerable enough in nothing but my underwear. I was just glad that I had chosen a black bra and matching panties that morning when I'd gotten dressed.

Lex seemed to appreciate my body as it was, but that only soothed my frazzled nerves a bit. I bit my bottom lip and knelt on the pillow, settling my bottom on my calves. I wasn't sure what to do with my hands, so I rested them on top of my thighs.

I chanced a glance up and nearly choked on my tongue. Lex had removed his jacket and unbuttoned the top three buttons of his shirt. In his hand was a set of padded wrist restraints and he was headed right toward me.

He didn't speak as he secured the restraints around my wrists in front of me. After he finished, he ran a finger under the material.

"Are these too tight?" he asked.

I shook my head.

His hand reached up and cupped my jaw firmly, forcing my face up so that I was looking into his eyes. "When I ask you a question, how should you respond?"

"N-no, Sir. They aren't too tight."

He gave me a small nod of approval. "I understand that this is all new to you, Ivie, but, if I have to remind you again, I will be using my hand on your bare ass."

I squirmed slightly at his threat. As always, Lex's keen eyes didn't miss a thing and he raised a single eyebrow.

"Are your hands numb or tingling?" he asked.

I almost shook my head, but remembered just in time. "No, Sir," I murmured.

He smiled slightly at me, then an inscrutable expression dropped over his face. One that made me very nervous.

Lex began to walk in a circle around my body, his hand lightly touching my shoulders as he moved. "Do you understand why you're here, little one?"

"No, Sir," I whispered. Well, I had an inkling, but I also had no idea why he brought me tonight.

"You did some things you shouldn't have." His fingers went from lightly tracing my shoulder into my hair. He gently gripped the back of my skull, tilting my head back so I had to look up the long line of his body to his face. "And now I'm going to punish you."

Every muscle from my belly button down contracted viciously at his words.

Then he leaned down and placed a chaste kiss on my lips before he continued, "And you will love every moment of it."

Before I could faint, which was a distinct possibility, he straightened and used the pressure of his hand cupping my nape as a cue for me to stand. I was a little awkward getting to my feet, but managed to do so without stumbling.

With his hand on the back of my neck, Lex led me to the spanking bench. As we drew to a halt, I shuddered. Oh shit. He didn't say a word as he positioned me and secured my hands to an O-ring in front of me. He used straps to secure my calves to the padded knee rests on each side of the bench. I was well and truly caught. He remained behind me and I couldn't turn my head to look at him, causing my anxiety level to rise even more.

His fingertips trailed down my spine, tracing each bump of my vertebrae, and leaving a trail of fire in their wake. When his hand reached my tailbone, he reversed direction.

"Since this is your first time in my dungeon, Ivie, I will use my hand. If you misbehave again, I will use a paddle."

I opened my mouth, then closed it with a quick snap. I wasn't supposed to speak unless he asked me a question, which he hadn't. Still, his threat caused a rush of heat between my legs rather than having the effect I expected, which was fear.

The damn vampire knew exactly what he was doing to me because he chuckled softly.

Suddenly, his fingers twisted into my underwear and he ripped them off me with a quick jerk. My entire body quaked. Oh God. He hadn't even really touched me yet and I felt like I was on the edge of an orgasm, which I hadn't thought possible. I always had difficulty climaxing, often to the frustration of my partners and myself.

I was distracted from my thoughts by the feel of his rough, hot palm cupping the cheek of my ass.

Lex hummed in the back of his throat. "Your skin is so pale, little one. It will be a pleasure to see it turn pink, then red, beneath my hand."

I squirmed again and his hand came down on my ass in a sharp slap.

"Keep still," he admonished.

I began to pant again. I didn't know if I could survive this.

His fingers began their leisurely travel up and down my spine again. "Do you know why you're being punished, Ivie?"

I was so caught up in the sensation of his hand on my bare skin, that I forgot his instructions and shook my head. Two short smacks on the fleshiest part of my bottom made me squeak. That stung. It didn't hurt badly, but it was enough to get my attention.

"No, Sir. I don't know why I'm being punished," I gasped.

His hand resumed its movement on my back. "You let another man touch you without my permission, Ivie. That is unacceptable."

I wanted to argue. That was ridiculous and sounded like a bull-shit excuse to me. Still, I wasn't in the position to be defiant, so I kept my mouth shut.

"Next time, I will ask you how many swats you think you deserve. This time, I will decide."

I swallowed the squeak that wanted to crawl up my throat.

"Though this is the first time you have misbehaved, your choice was a very bad one. I think that we will start with ten."

I sighed, thinking that ten didn't sound like that many. At least he hadn't chosen fifteen, or, God forbid, twenty. I twitched slightly as his hand began to caress my backside, squeezing and molding my flesh.

"You will count them for me aloud," he said. "And you will call me Sir. Do you understand?"

"Yes, Sir," I answered.

Suddenly, the loud crack of his palm meeting my skin filled the room and my entire body went rigid. Holy fucking shit, that hurt! His hand had come down directly on one of my cheeks.

"Ivie," he prompted.

"One, Sir," I choked.

The next slap wasn't quite as hard, but it still stung, and it was centered over my other ass cheek.

"Two, Sir."

After the fourth swat, I wasn't sure I could make it to ten. My ass felt like it was on fire. When I reached six, the burning sensation on my bottom had spread to my pussy. By the eighth blow, I was struggling against my bonds to raise my ass in order to meet his hand.

Lex paused after the ninth blow. I whimpered. Even though the skin of my ass ached, I needed that final blow. The pain had mixed so thoroughly with the pleasure that I couldn't recognize either clearly. Finally, when I thought I would lose my mind, Lex brought his hand down on both my cheeks.

I shuddered against the spanking bench, desperate to come but not able to cross the line alone.

"Ten, Sir," I moaned.

In less than five seconds, Lex had released my legs and hands and was carrying me to the bed with an arm behind my back and another under my knees. Setting me on my feet, he unhooked my bra and stripped it off my arms before he tossed me on the sheets. Lex was on top of me before I managed to get my bearings.

Quickly, he grabbed my arms and lifted my hands above my head. I twisted to watch as he snapped my restraints to another small O-ring hidden at the top of the mattress. Panting, I tossed my hair out of my face, my legs moving restlessly against the sheets. The smooth fabric beneath me was cool against my burning skin, but it felt rough under my abused ass.

I watched in silence as Lex climbed off the bed and literally ripped his shirt from his body. My eyes followed every bulge and flex of his muscles as he stripped the material down his arms and dropped it on the floor. He toed off his shoes and socks and started on the buckle of his belt. I licked my lips with anticipation.

As suddenly as he began his striptease, Lex stopped, his hands going to his hips as he eyed me speculatively. Leaving his belt undone, he turned and began walking away from me.

I almost called out to him, but bit my tongue. I didn't know what he was doing or planning, but I did know that I didn't want to fuck this up. I had to trust him. I watched in silence as he took another set of restraints off the wall and brought them to the bed. There were two thick straps that looked like larger versions of my wrist cuffs and two longer, thinner straps attached to the top of those.

Smiling that same wicked smile he'd given me outside, Lex wrapped one of the thicker pieces around my thigh. The thin strap was attached to the top. He repeated the process with my other leg. Just as I realized what he was planning and started to protest, he grabbed both the thinner straps and attached them to the headboard on either side of the O-ring my hands were clipped on. This act brought my knees up almost to my chest and spread legs wide, leaving me horribly vulnerable.

My wide eyes met his, and that devilish smile never left his face. "Perfect," he growled.

His eyes drifted down my naked torso to my pussy. He never looked away as he climbed off the bed and finished unbuttoning and unzipping his pants. I watched as he stripped off his pants and underwear, leaving him naked. And what a sight it was.

There was naked, then there was extra special, *that isn't gonna fit* naked. My pussy spasmed at the thought of him trying to slide that monster inside me. After the spanking, however, I was game to try.

Never taking his eyes off the area between my thighs, Lex crawled across the bed to me. I couldn't help shifting under his stare. Was he going to do what I thought he was?

As his face drew level with my pussy, he leaned down and nipped my inner thigh. Yes, I realized he was going to do what I thought.

Still looking at my most private places, Lex spoke. "I have wondered for months about this, Ivie."

I looked down my nude body at him, struggling not to writhe on the bed like a nymphomaniac at the image of his face right between my thighs.

He traced a finger over my clit and I almost screamed. After the spanking, my girl parts felt as though they were a hundred times more sensitive than usual. "I wondered how you would taste."

I moaned, letting my head fall back. Then his tongue swiped over my clit and my back arched. I couldn't move much, but my hips tried to buck as he devoured my pussy. He licked and sucked as though he were starving for the taste of me. In less than a minute, I felt my orgasm bearing down on me like a rocket. It was going to be huge. Just as the tingles in my clit began to signal my oncoming climax, Lex pulled his mouth away from me and blew lightly.

I groaned loudly, thrashing against my restraints. I wanted to scream and curse, but I bit down hard on my bottom lip. Somehow, I remembered that I wasn't supposed to speak unless he asked me a question. How I did that, I had no clue because I could barely remember my own name.

Lex levered himself over my body, sliding his cock over my clit in a slow, firm motion. I tried to close my thighs around his hips but I was bound too tightly. His eyes were almost so bright I thought I would burn to ash under their intensity.

His mouth crashed down on mine and I could taste myself on his lips. His tongue thrust into my mouth as his hips moved against mine in a slow, maddening dance. Lex nipped my bottom lip before moving down my neck, grazing the skin with his teeth. I thrashed beneath him, too caught up in the tsunami of my desire to try and control my movements.

Then his lips closed around one of my nipples, sucking hard. I cried out, arching my back into the intense sensation. His teeth bit delicately into my breast without breaking the skin before he moved to the other one. As he continued to torture my nipples with his teeth, he never stopped sliding the thick, pulsing length of his cock against my drenched center, bumping my clit with each stroke.

Just before I was about to explode into a thousand bits, Lex stopped and knelt between my thighs.

"Please," I whimpered.

He seemed absorbed with the sight of the crown of his cock rubbing lightly against my clit. Still, he responded.

"Please what, Ivie?" he asked.

"I need you," I whispered. And I did. I needed to feel that thick, long, beautiful dick thrusting inside me more than I needed my next breath.

His hand lightly slapped my pussy and I gasped at the heat that streaked through my extremities. Then his fingers dipped inside my drenched opening.

Lex lifted his eyes to mine as his fingers crooked inside me, pressing firmly against that special place inside me that made me feel like my skin was going to split in two.

"Who does this pussy belong to?" he asked.

I answered without a single hesitation. "You."

He grinned that diabolical grin again. "Who do you belong to?" he demanded, his fingers sliding in and out of me, first two, then three, stretching me until I felt a slight burn.

My head whipped against the sheets at the sensations he was creating in my body. Again, he lightly slapped my clit, but this time with his other hand. I screamed.

"Answer me, Ivie," he growled.

"You! I belong to you!" I cried.

As soon as I said it, the head of his cock replaced his fingers and he began to push inside me. I froze, barely breathing, as he pushed in an inch. Lex pulled out slightly, then thrust deeper. He repeated the motion three more times before he was seated fully inside me.

I knew he was large, but my pussy burned as it stretched to accommodate him. As though he sensed my distress, Lex pressed a thumb against my wet clit and began to draw firm circles. Within seconds, I relaxed around him, only to tighten again as he began a long slide out of me.

Lex groaned and forged back into my body, deep and slow. Then he did it again. I tried to lift my hips, to urge him on with my body, but he wouldn't have any part of it. He continued to massage my clit as his thrusts became deeper, harder, and faster.

"Are you going to come on my cock, Ivie?" he asked in a deep, gravelly voice that made tingles dance down my spine.

I gasped and writhed beneath him, but didn't answer. His hand stopped moving on my clit and snaked up my torso to pinch my nipple. The sharp pain traveled straight down my abdomen to the place where our bodies were joined.

"Answer me," he commanded.

"Yes! Yes, Sir!" I cried.

His thumb was suddenly on my clit again, pressing in deeper and harder, moving more quickly.

Then the orgasm he had denied me twice before detonated within me with the force of a nuclear bomb. My entire body seized, my head flying back, and I screamed. My entire being was focused on the feeling of his cock between my legs and his hand on my center.

"Oh fuck," he groaned, his thrusts becoming short and jerky and I knew he was coming with me.

He slowed the movement of his body within mine, as my pussy contracted around him from the aftershocks of my devastating orgasm. As my body quieted, Lex pulled out of me gently and I quivered at the sensation of his cock leaving my body.

Inexplicably, my eyelids grew heavy. I was already drifting as he unhooked my legs from the headboard and removed the thigh straps. My arms tingled as he loosened the wrist cuffs and lowered my arms, massaging my shoulders and biceps gently.

The last thing I remembered before sleep claimed me, was the feel of his hot, naked body curving around my back and his arms wrapping around me tightly.

Chapter Thirteen

SOMETIME LATER, I woke up with Lex's mouth latched on my neck as he slid a hand between my legs. Still drowsy, I arched my back, grinding my ass against his cock. He groaned and nipped my throat lightly. As my arousal increased, he rolled me onto my stomach, lifting my arms above my head and using one hand to pin my wrists down to the mattress. Then he slipped his fingers from between my thighs and his hard cock replaced it.

I squirmed and moaned beneath him as he worked his length into me. Flat on my stomach, with my legs so close together, it was an extremely tight fit. When he bottomed out inside me, Lex withdrew and began to thrust hard and deep. I gasped as every muscle in my body tensed. Within minutes, I hovered on the edge of what promised to be a fantastic, toe-curling orgasm. I tried to thrust back against him, to encourage him to go faster.

Lex merely laughed softly in my ear and used his strong thighs to force my legs together. I was stretched out on my stomach, arms and legs pinned. Finally, he moved forward until he was straddling my hips. When he moved, the angle of his penetration changed and I saw stars. After two more thrusts, I turned my head, sank my teeth into his bicep, and came hard.

Lex growled against my shoulder, his teeth sinking in so deeply I was sure he had broken the skin, and pounded into me. I knew I would be bruised. Moments later, I felt him shudder against me with his own release.

He stilled over me, resting most of his weight on my back.

"Can't breathe," I gasped.

Lex grunted and rolled off of me. I shifted slightly, trying to catch my breath and I grimaced at the size of the wet spot beneath me. Then reality raised up and bit me right on the ass. Oh God, he hadn't used a condom. Either time. Oh fucking, fucking, *motherfucking* hell.

When my body tensed, Lex turned his head to look at me in the dim light of his play room. He must have turned off most of the other lights sometime before, I thought inanely.

"What's wrong, little one?" he asked, rubbing a hand down my spine.

I tossed my hair out of my face and glared at him. "You didn't use a rubber!"

Lex looked at me as though I had lost my mind. "What?"

"A condom, a glove, a fucking prophylactic!" My voice rose with each word.

He stared at me blankly then threw his head back and roared with laughter. I barely refrained from smacking him on the chest. While I was almost certain he wasn't angry with me any longer, I didn't want to push my luck.

"I don't understand how you can find this so funny," I snapped. "For all I know I could have some half-vampire growing inside me, waiting to eat its way out of my uterus! Or a freaky disease! I never, *never* have sex without protection unless my partner has had a health exam first!"

His laughter died immediately and his chocolate brown eyes pierced me with laser-like intensity.

"You find the idea of my child distasteful?" he asked, his voice dangerously soft.

I was too wigged out to be scared of his tone. "No! I find the thought of dying at the fangs of my hypothetical infant distasteful. One, because I don't want to die. Two, because I don't want my imaginary child to grow up thinking that they killed me!"

It wasn't until Lex's face relaxed after my words that I realized how he interpreted my fit. With my eyes huge, I shook my head at him. "I didn't mean that as a slur against vampires, Lex. I'm freaking out here!"

He rolled me over so that I was lying on my back and he leaned over me, a slight smile on his face. "Well, calm yourself. You won't be having any hybrid babies. I can't get you pregnant as long as you're human." I swallowed hard because that meant he could knock me up if I became a vampire, which I wasn't sure I wanted to do. "And vampires don't carry disease. Our bodies are immune to all sexual illnesses. We can smell it in the blood and avoid drinking from infected humans unless we have no other choice. Ill people don't taste very good."

My eyes bugged out of my head even more. That was more than I needed to know.

He pushed my hair off my face. "I promise that you are safe with me, Ivie," he said earnestly.

I shook my head. "I can't think about this right now. If I do, I will lose my shit."

Lex smiled. "I have the perfect distraction."

I looked at him expectantly.

"A shower."

Honestly, that sounded good because I was a mess. But I had one question first.

"Can we drop the 'Sir' stuff for a while?" I asked. "I think you've blown my mind enough for one evening."

He laughed and squeezed my waist. "How about this, unless we're in this room or I tell you that you must call me Sir, you don't have to say it?"

I nodded, then remembered that we were still in the dungeon and added a cheeky, "Yes, Sir."

Lex chuckled and climbed out of the bed before he plucked me off the sheets. He threw me over his shoulder like a damn sack of potatoes and carried me, naked, up two flights of stairs and into his bathroom.

"I can walk, you know," I complained as he leaned over to place my feet on the tile.

I forgot all about my complaint as I looked around the huge bathroom. It was half the size of my apartment.

"Maybe I just enjoy carrying you," he murmured as he leaned into the glass-encased shower.

I watched as he turned on three showerheads. I decided then and there that this bathroom would be mine from now on. If Lex tried to get rid of me, I'd just have to tie him up in his own dungeon so I could keep the use of his shower.

He nudged me through the door and under the hot water. As soon as the liquid hit my sore and well-used body, I closed my eyes and sighed in contentment. These showerheads were fantastic.

"What are you thinking about right now?" he asked.

I opened one eye and stared at him. "How much I love your showerheads," I answered. "And trying to figure out a way to trap you in your dungeon so I can use this shower whenever I want."

He smirked. "All you have to do is ask," he said simply.

"Sorry, I'm not asking. You might say no. I'm telling you. Shower. Mine."

Lex chuckled and stepped in, lining his body up behind me. His hands slid around my waist, pulling me tight against him. I felt his lips touch the side of my neck before they moved up to my ear.

"Haven't you realized I can't tell you no, little one?" His voice was low, gravelly, and I felt it all over my body.

I started to turn around but Lex stilled the movement. He stepped back, but used one hand on my hip to keep me in place. I heard the top of a bottle click open, Lex's other hand disappeared. I waited and then I felt his hands in my hair. My head fell back and I groaned as he massaged shampoo into my hair and scalp. It felt fantastic. I let him wash and condition my hair, then wash my body, feeling both relaxed and turned on simultaneously. I turned when he was done helping me rinse and placed both hands on his chest.

"Your turn," I said.

He stood still as I reached up, pressing my breasts against his chest as I washed his hair. I had him tilt his head back under the spray of one of the heads, then I took the washcloth and soap. After I worked up a good lather, I began to run the cloth all over his gorgeous body. I noticed scars. Lots of scars. I used my fingertips to learn each curve of his heavily muscled shoulders, down his chest and the ridges of his abdomen. Then I moved down to his legs. I washed the firm muscle of his ass, before moving around to the front.

The one place on his body I hadn't cleaned was hard, long, and ready to go. I traced his hip muscles with the fingers of each hand, starting at the top of the V shape and following the line down to his cock. The clear definition of his muscles was an invitation to touch.

When I reached my destination, washing him gently, Lex reached down and pulled me up by my wrists. I squeaked when he lifted me by my ass and pressed me against the shower wall.

"You can play later. I don't have the patience right now." With those words, he angled his cock into my center and let my weight drop slowly until I was impaled.

This time, our coupling was fast and furious. My climax started at my scalp and rolled downward in a vicious wave. Only Lex's hand fisted in my hair kept me from smashing my skull against the hard tile behind me.

After I caught my breath, he pulled out of me slowly and lowered me to my feet. He had to help support me as he turned off the water, helped me out of the shower, and wrapped me in a huge bath sheet. I wondered why in the hell vampires seemed to have an inclination for towels the size of a blanket.

After he dried us off, he pulled me into the bedroom behind him. A glance at the alarm clock on his bedside table showed it was 3 a.m. He yanked the comforter down and I fell on to the most comfortable mattress ever created. I pulled the sheet and blanket over my naked body as Lex went back to turn off the bathroom light.

By the time he returned to the bed and climbed in behind me, I was dead to the world.

✧   ✧   ✧

MY LITTLE BUBBLE of happiness burst after I woke up later that morning. I opened my eyes and realized I was in Lex's huge bed alone. Bleary-eyed, I looked around in the light of day and saw that his room was masculine and simple, with sand colored walls, dark wooden furniture, and a comforter the color of merlot spread over me. I noticed my clothes folded neatly on the end of the bed.

Feeling a little off-balance, I climbed out of the bed and dressed. I wandered into the bathroom and found a selection of women's toiletries and a brand spanking new toothbrush, still in the package, on the counter for me.

That off-balance feeling transformed into a rock in the pit of my stomach. While I appreciated that Lex went to the trouble of ensuring that I would have everything I would need to be comfortable and clean in the morning, it also made me wonder how many other women had found themselves in the exact position I was in now.

My mellow mood was crushed. I brushed my teeth and washed my face on autopilot, then I twisted my hair into a messy knot at the nape of my neck. I could barely meet my own eyes in the mirror because I couldn't believe that I was so naive. Lex was hundreds of years old. Of course he would probably see sex more casually than I would.

I took a deep breath and reminded myself not to be jealous or hurt. No other woman was here now. He was with me. For now. I shook my head and shoved those words out of my mind. There was no guarantee in any relationship at the beginning.

I had to smile at myself. I needed to chill out. Obviously frequent and amazing sex turned me into a lunatic. Then again, I probably hated the idea that my relationship with Lex might not be long term because he'd ruined me for all other men. I don't see how any man could make me feel the way he had the night before. Hell, several of my previous boyfriends could barely manage to bring me to orgasm once in one night, much less three times.

Rolling my eyes at my own crazy train of thought, I left the bathroom and headed downstairs. Since Lex hadn't exactly given me a tour that last time I was at his house, I followed my instincts. There was a hall to the right of the doorway. I padded toward the end of it in my bare feet. I glanced in the rooms that I passed and saw a library and a large formal dining room. They were both empty.

As I approached the last door, I smelled coffee and my mouth began to water. I pushed open the kitchen door and stopped short. Lex was standing in the kitchen wearing nothing but a pair of black men's pajama pants. His arms were crossed over his chest and he was smiling.

When I was finally able to tear my eyes away from the sight he presented, I saw a petite blonde woman standing at the sink wearing a snug pair of tiny cutoff shorts and a blood red tank top. Her long hair was pulled up in a ponytail on the crown of her head. She had turned to face me and was staring at me as though she had seen a ghost. And she was gorgeous.

My entire body felt as though it were dipped in ice water. I had just been wondering about Lex's other women and it appeared I was face-to-face with one.

I stepped back and glanced at Lex. He was frowning at me. I tried not to meet either of their eyes.

"I can see I'm interrupting. Um, I'll just…." I didn't finish the sentence. I turned on my bare foot and went right back out the kitchen door.

I was almost to the front door when Lex caught me. I wasn't sure what I planned to do when I got outside other than get the hell away from this house. His hand caught my elbow and swung me around to face him.

"Ivie, what in the hell just happened?" he demanded.

I tried to pull my arm out of his grasp, but Lex held fast. "I can't do this."

"Can't do what?" He seemed genuinely bewildered. "What is the problem?"

I eyed him suspiciously. He was remaining true to his word. He wasn't even attempting to read my thoughts. Unfortunately, that meant I had to have this uncomfortable conversation.

I rubbed my temples. "It's the women's toiletries in the bathroom."

He looked even more confused, but edging toward annoyed. "Pardon?"

I sighed and forced myself to meet his eyes. "When I saw all those women's things in your bathroom this morning, plus the fresh toothbrush, it just hit me a little harder than I expected."

Lex's eyes narrowed. "Explain."

"That I'm one of many," I whispered.

Lex just stared at me for a moment, his eyes burning with black fire. It scared me a little. It was the same look he had last night when he saw me watching movies with Finn.

"Do you want some more coffee, Lex?"

My eyes flicked away from the angry vampire to look at the thin, shapely blonde standing at the mouth of the hall.

"No, thank you, Bridget. Go ahead and go home for the day. I'll compensate you for your time."

She bit her lip and nodded before she turned and went back down the hall.

I watched her and felt my pulse accelerating. Lex was still watching me, unmoving. He didn't even blink. His scary demeanor made me fidget and bite my lower lip.

"Just who do you think Bridget is to me, Ivie?" he asked.

I blinked, not expecting the question. "Um, I don't know," I murmured.

"That's right," he said, nodding. "You don't know, because you didn't ask me." He turned away from me suddenly, dragging his hands through his hair, cursing loudly. He whirled around and came directly at me.

I just managed not to flinch and stand my ground as he got right in my space, lowering his head to get eye-to-eye with me.

"Bridget is my housekeeper. She is not now, and never has been, my lover."

"Oh," I whispered.

His eyes were still burning so hot I was surprised my eyebrows weren't singed. "And the toiletries you seem so concerned about, the ones I placed in the bathroom so you would be comfortable and clean if you wished, I keep on hand for political guests." He let me digest this for a moment. "Did it occur to you that I am a Council member? I have leaders from other vampire nations here all the time. Even the most organized minds forget essentials from time to time."

I felt a hot blush crawl up my cleavage and neck to my face. Oh, shit. I had misunderstood the situation completely. Mortification kept me silent.

Lex cupped my cheeks with both hands, his eyes no longer as angry, but still hot. "You are very lucky that you have bruises this morning, or we would be down in the dungeon right now."

I just looked at him. There was only one thing to do.

"I'm so sorry, Lex. I assumed the worst after I found all those beauty products in your bathroom, including a new toothbrush, and then I saw Bridget. I thought you were just adding me to your collection of women. You know, thin and blonde, fat and brunette."

The last of the anger left his eyes at my words. Instead they were just a little sad. He pressed his lips to my forehead. When he pulled away slightly, he said, "I wish I could find every man or woman who has ever undermined your self-esteem, little one. You are a beautiful woman and I would not be so certain of that if you changed a single thing about yourself."

His words seemed sincere. I realized that he really did come from a different time and he had lived through centuries when the standard of beauty was completely different. To him, I really was beautiful.

That knowledge put a crack in the wall I'd built around my heart when it came to this vampire. I stepped closer to him and rose onto my tiptoes. I placed my lips on his, knowing that I was in more danger than ever before because I was well on my way to falling in love with someone who would want to change me irrevocably.

Chapter Fourteen

A
FTER LEX DEALT with my mini meltdown, he took me into the kitchen and sat me at the counter. He made me a cup of coffee exactly the way I liked it, then he cooked an omelet and toast for our breakfast. As we sat at the little table in the breakfast nook, I looked at Lex and grinned.

"Are all male vampires so domesticated?" I teased. "Conner cooks a lot, and now you."

Lex grinned at me and I forgot what we were talking about. His smile was fantastic and completely transformed his face. "Don't get your hopes up, little one. Omelets, spaghetti, and grilled meats are the extent of my cooking abilities."

I took a bite of the extremely delicious omelet. "Well, it's good. I don't cook."

"You don't?" he asked.

I shook my head.

"Your mother didn't teach you?"

I grinned at him as I put my fork down and grabbed my coffee cup. "Oh, I didn't say I can't cook, only that I don't."

He chuckled.

I took a sip of my coffee. There was something that I wondered about, but I was hesitant to ask. I mean, I didn't know anything about vampire etiquette, so I hoped I didn't offend him. I had to ask though, because he seemed to be in a really good mood and I wanted to know.

"Um, Lex, I have a question," I said.

His eyes were their usual dark chocolate color and they twinkled. "Okay."

"It's about vampires and, well, biting."

He nodded.

I sucked in a deep breath and prepared to dive in headfirst. "Okay, so I was just wondering....why haven't you bitten me? I mean, I'm not asking you to or anything, but, from some of the things Donna has told me, I'm curious."

Lex's attention was so focused on me, I thought for a moment I could feel the heat of his eyes on my face as he studied me. Finally, he broke eye contact and took my hand, looking at my fingers.

"Taking blood is an intimate and intense experience for both a vampire and a human," he began. "You've been so nervous around me, always looking for a reason to run away, I didn't want to give you any more ammunition."

I stared at him with wide eyes. He was absolutely right. I was looking for reasons to run away, before and now. He scared the ever-loving shit out of me, so some part of me was looking for any excuse.

He looked back into my eyes, still toying with my fingers. "Did you enjoy my fucking you last night?" he asked, point blank.

I really shouldn't like his blunt talk, but I felt a tingle between my legs when he said the word, 'fucking', and the memories it evoked. I nodded.

Somehow, without being obvious, he shifted forward slightly. "Well, if I had bitten you, your climax would have been longer and more intense. Usually, the first time, a human partner will pass out from the ecstasy."

I swallowed hard. He was absolutely right. If he had bitten me last night and I had come so hard that I fainted, my ass would have left a trail of fire behind me as I ran for the door. I quivered as his hand came up and brushed my neck right above my collarbone. It felt like a threat, and a promise. I felt it shoot from the skin at my throat to my nipples then my clit.

His face filled my vision. "I will bite you, Ivie. I don't even have to read your mind to be able to tell that you want it. I can see it just by looking at you. Your pupils are larger, your nipples are hard." He closed his eyes and inhaled. When he lifted his lids, his irises were glowing like two dark, golden topazes. "I can even smell it. You smell sweet and just a little spicy. I'm sure your blood will taste the same."

I felt a rush of heat between my legs and realized that, with just his words, I was ready for him to fuck me blind. I watched as his mouth curved into that same evil smile, as though he knew exactly what he was doing to me but had no plans to put me out of my misery.

"The next time we make love," he said, straightening, moving away from me, "I will bite you and taste every part of you." He glanced at his watch as though his promise had no effect on him whatsoever. "Now, it's almost ten. We should go pick up your things from Conner's."

I blinked at him. "What?"

His gazed shifted back to me and he looked a little wary. As well he should, because I hoped I had just misunderstood him but, somehow, I knew I hadn't.

"We need to get your things from Conner's house," he repeat- ed. "Unless you don't mind not having a spare set of clothes for the time you are living here."

"Living here?" I repeated, my eyes narrowing.

"Yes, living here." His voice was testy.

"I don't recall agreeing to move in," I began. "Actually, I don't even recall being asked if I wanted to move."

Lex gave me that stare again, the one that clearly said he thought I was a few IQ points shy of reasonably intelligent. "What?"

I rose from the table, my fragile enjoyment of the morning fraying rapidly. "You can't just say we're going to get my things from Conner and Donna's house and assume I'll go along with the plan. I'm a twenty-nine year old woman, not a stray kitten."

Lex sighed and seemed to understand my point. "Okay, will you please move in here?" he asked politely.

I shook my head. "No."

His expression turned thunderous. "What did you say?" he whispered.

I scowled at him, refusing to back down even though he intim- idated the hell out of me. Crossing my arms over my chest, I leaned forward until we were almost nose-to-nose.

"I said, no! No, I won't go to Conner and Donna's and pick up my things. No to living here with you right now. No!" I resisted sticking my tongue out at him, but just barely. Something about his high handed manner just drove me nuts.

I also needed time to think about the idea of him biting me. The nasty vamp bastard who had kidnapped Donna and me had bitten me and it *hurt*. From the things Donna told me later, after it was all over, made me think that perhaps this wasn't the norm. I mean, before Conner turned her, Donna said she begged him to bite her during sex, so it must be kind of nice.

Still, the whole idea of literally putting my life in someone's hands while I was rolling around naked with them made me very nervous. I wasn't sure I could go through with it.

Lex rose from his seat. "You will stay here where I can protect you."

I tilted my head back, refusing to be intimidated by his looming over me like a dark shadow. "I hate to bring this up, but you've been gone more than you've been here the last month. I'm sure you'll have to leave again at some point. How are you going to protect me? At least Conner has extra men at his house," I argued.

Lex glowered at me. "I'm also a member of the Council and I can acquire men if the need arises. I want you here."

I shook my head vehemently. "No. I either go back to Donna's or I go back to my apartment," I argued.

His hands clamped on my upper arms. "Do you understand the kind of danger you're in?" he asked angrily. "There are vampires out there who want to hurt Conner and me. If they figure out how much you mean to me, they will use you, possibly even kill you."

I was intrigued by his mention of how much I meant to him, but first, I needed to address his high-handed attitude. I enjoyed his dominating me in the bedroom, or dungeon, but, when it came to my life choices, my decisions were my own, not his. If he wanted me to stay with him, he really needed to work on convincing me it was the right thing to do.

Lex's hands tore through his hair. "Goddammit!" he yelled. "Why do you have to be so fucking stubborn?"

I shrugged. "That's just the way I am."

He put his face in mine, something he habitually did when he wanted his own way. I noticed it before and realized he did it a lot when we were arguing. I wasn't sure if he was doing it on purpose. Whether he realized it or not, Lex tried to physically intimidate me into doing what he wanted. We would have to discuss that at a later date, because, at that moment, there was only one battle I was interested in winning.

"Well, maybe the way things should be is for me to haul your pretty, white ass down to the dungeon, strap you to a table, and cut all your clothes off of you," he growled.

While the image that popped into my head made my clit and nipples perk up, the rest of me was pissed at the thought.

"Lex, I am not ready for a step like that."

"I'm not asking you to move in. I'm telling you that you're going to do it. It's for your safety. If you want your own goddamn room, you can have it. I want you safe!" he roared.

Obviously, my hard-line approach wasn't working. I decided to try a different tactic. "Why is my safety so important to you? We don't know each other that well. Hell, we just had sex for the first time last night. You're acting more like an overprotective father than a new boyfriend."

I kept my voice calm, but my words seemed to enrage him further. His hands grabbed my arms, pulling me up on my toes.

"Boyfriend?" He spat the word as though it made him sick.

I stared at him wide-eyed. I had no response. He gave me a little shake and I gasped. Oh God, he was pissed.

"What we have between us is more than that. Surely, you can't be that blind."

My hands curled around his forearms. Even angry he hadn't hurt me, though I was pretty sure he was strong enough to crush my biceps with a slight flex of his hand. As though he were reading my thoughts, his fingers squeezed a little tighter. I winced because, though it wasn't that hard, some of my skin was pinched by the change in his grip.

Lex saw my flinch and released my arms. "I'm sorry."

I shook my head. "I'm okay. My skin just got a little pinched."

He lifted the sleeve of my t-shirt and we both looked at the skin of my arm. There was a red mark that was rapidly turning purple. Crap, I always did seem to bruise easily. The pinch hadn't even hurt that badly.

I glanced at Lex and saw that his face was tight.

"I'm so sorry, little one. I didn't mean to harm you." He started to touch the spot with a finger but stopped before he made contact with my skin.

I grabbed his hand and squeezed it gently. "You didn't really hurt me, Lex. I just bruise easily. Sometimes, I barely bump a piece of furniture and end up with a huge purple mark on my leg."

He still appeared extremely upset. "I shouldn't have put my hands on you. I am deeply sorry."

Great, I was sure that he was preparing for self-flagellation. I had an idea to distract him.

"So, do you feel badly enough to take me back to Donna's and let me stay there?"

He started to nod, then his eyes snapped to mine and narrowed. "Did you just try to manipulate me?" he asked menacingly.

I had to fight a smile as I shook my head.

The distress on Lex's face began to melt. "Are you sure I didn't hurt you?" he asked again.

I nodded.

"Then, no, you can't stay with Donna. And I will be punishing you for your behavior later."

Now that he was calmer, I decided to try and continue our discussion. Maybe he would listen to reason. "Lex, I'm serious. I don't think I'm ready to move in here with you."

He lifted a hand and I didn't finish what I wanted to say because he didn't look angry any longer, only determined.

"You will stay here. If you continue to argue, instead of the ten swats I intend to give you, it will be fifteen. Then twenty. I'm sure you understand where this is going."

I huffed out a breath. "You can't force me to stay here," I argued.

Lex studied me. "Yes, I can. I could bind you to my St. Andrew's Cross downstairs and have Donna pack your things. I'm sure Conner would be happy to send them over with a couple of his men."

"You're crazy! Why would you think that would be okay?"

His eyes were those of a predator now, calculating, aloof, but no longer angry. He fisted his hand in my hair, another habit of his that I had noticed. When he wanted my attention, that's what he did. This one I kind of liked, even though I would never willingly admit it.

"Because you're mine," he answered. "You told me yourself last night."

I clenched my jaw so tightly, I thought I might crack a few of my teeth. I couldn't argue with that, because it was the truth. I should have known that would come back and bite me on the ass.

"Fine," I snapped. "I would like to go get my things today."

I could tell that the asshole was trying not to grin at my grudging agreement and he nodded.

The almost smile that hovered in his eyes disappeared quickly. "Thank you, Ivie."

I sighed. I couldn't maintain my anger with such sincere grati-
tude and concern. Even though I didn't like it, I also understood
that Lex wanted me to stay with him because he thought it was for
my own good.

I needed more coffee first. Donna was going to give me hell
about this.

Chapter Fifteen

A S IT TURNED OUT, I was right. Donna gave me hell when I showed up, but not for the reason I thought. Lex called Conner while he was driving us over to let them know we were coming to pick up my things.

I could hear Conner chuckling and Donna bitching from the passenger seat. After Lex hung up, I asked, "What's Donna's deal?"

He looked at me, his eyes sparkling with humor. "Apparently, Conner had to call Finn this morning to ask if you were with him when you never came downstairs."

"Oh crap," I muttered.

He grinned. "Finn explained some of what happened last night."

"Oh crap."

Lex laughed.

When we pulled up in front of Conner's house, I saw Donna standing on the porch, her arms crossed over her torso and a toe tapping.

"God, she looks like my mother," I mumbled.

Donna's scowl deepened as though she heard me.

"I think she heard you," Lex said.

"Shit on toast."

I opened the passenger door of Lex's SUV and hopped down. Donna waited, with a disapproving look on her face, until I got to the top of the steps leading to the front door of the McMansion.

"You couldn't leave a note or spare a minute to phone me?" Donna asked, looking every inch someone's mother. The disapproving look on her face was almost a spot-on impression of my mother.

"Sorry, Mom. I was a little busy."

The tight line of her mouth relaxed a little and humor sparkled in her eyes. Bitch was fucking with me. "Oh, I just bet you were."

In spite of myself, I felt a blush creep up my cleavage to my face. Damn my fair skin. I brushed past Donna and stuck my tongue out at her as I went by. Her laughter followed me up the stairs to the guest room where I had been sleeping until last night.

A few minutes later, as I was folding up clothes and packing my suitcase, Donna stuck her head in the door.

"Is it safe to enter?" she asked.

I rolled my eyes at her and kept packing.

"I come bearing gifts." She walked into the room, carrying a bottle of wine and two glasses.

"We're drinking at 10:30 in the morning?" I asked.

She glanced at the bottle. "Yeah, want me to get the champagne and OJ?"

I shook my head. "Fuck it. Fill that glass up for me."

After Donna filled up a glass with chilled white wine, she handed it to me. Then she filled her own and took a sip. She shuddered.

"Ugh. White just isn't my thing."

I tasted it. It was delicious. "This is good stuff. What's wrong with you?"

Donna set the glass on the nightstand by the bed and flopped down next to my suitcase on the bed. "I brought it for you. You know I like red wine the best."

I took huge sip. "Well, thanks," I mumbled.

Donna rolled onto her side and bent her arm at the elbow, resting her head on her palm. "So, did you and Lex talk at all, or were you too busy doing other things?"

I almost choked on my wine. Shit, I should have known that she wanted dirt.

"We talked," I answered vaguely.

"About?"

I sighed. "We talked about me moving in with him. Well, actually, we argued. Then we talked about the whole biting thing."

Donna perked up. "He hasn't bitten you yet?" she asked.

I shook my head.

"Oh, girl, you are in for a treat! I swear it's the most intense feeling. Your orgasms are going to be mind-blowing."

I laughed softly. "If they got any more mind-blowing, I'd be dead."

Donna grinned. "So, is he into kink?"

Cursing my fair skin, I blushed again.

She threw her head back and howled with laughter. "You should see the look on your face! Oh my God, he must be very kinky for that kind of reaction."

I glanced toward the closed bedroom door and leaned forward. I didn't want to risk Lex or Conner overhearing this conversation.

"He strapped me down to a bench and spanked me last night," I whispered. "Then he cuffed me to his bed and strapped my thighs down. I've never come that hard before."

Donna's eyes glazed over. "Holy shit. I'm not big on spanking but that sounds hot."

I took a sip of my chilled white wine because it had been hot. So hot in fact, that the memory made my clothes feel too heavy and tight.

Her expression changed slightly. "So, did the two of you discuss anything else?"

I shook my head.

Donna smiled slightly. "So he didn't talk about Claiming you?"

I stared at her in horror, then remembered that I needed to be careful how I reacted. By then it was too late.

"What is it?" she asked, sitting up straight on the bed. "Did he scare you? Or are you not serious about him, because, Ivie, you need to know Lex is—"

I interrupted her. "Even if he was interested in that, I'm not."

Donna fell silent and stared at me for a moment. "Okay, don't get mad, I'm not trying to read you, but, Ivie, you are putting off some seriously agitated vibes."

"I can't talk about this, Dee," I said, trying to evade the subject.

"Ivie, you know you can tell me anything. What's going on?"

I sighed and began pacing the floor by the bed. Crap, I didn't want to have this discussion with her because I knew it would bother her and, no matter what she was, she was first and foremost my friend. I didn't want to hurt her.

"Even if he was serious, hell, even if I loved him, I wouldn't want to be Claimed."

Donna looked confused. "Why?"

I threw my hands up in the air, annoyed and afraid that I was about to lose one of my closest friends. "I won't commit to someone who wants to change me on a fundamental level."

Her eyebrows lowered. "I don't understand."

I sat down on the bench at the end of the bed, sighing heavily. "Donna, he would eventually want to change me into a vampire, as though being human isn't good enough. I mean, think about a few weeks ago when Conner and Lex said they couldn't tell me what was going on because I am human and vulnerable to manipulation by vampires. I don't want to be with someone who won't view me as an equal partner in the relationship. Just because I enjoy being bossed around in the bedroom, doesn't mean that I want that in the rest of my life."

When I finished my impassioned mini speech, I looked over at my friend. She was studying me intently and looked surprisingly calm. In fact, she didn't seem hurt in the slightest by my comments about vampires.

"Do you like it when a man opens your door for you?" she asked.

"What?" What did that have to do with anything?

"Do you?" she prompted.

I nodded.

"Okay, do you like it when he walks you to your door? Or changes your flat tire?"

I nodded again, still unsure where this was going.

"If a man says he wants to protect you and take care of you, are you offended?"

I was beginning to get an idea where this was going and I wasn't sure I was going to like it. "No, I'm not offended."

She leaned forward. "If a man told you he wanted to spend eternity with you, would you feel as though he saw you as inadequate?"

Goddammit, she had a point. "No, I wouldn't think that."

Looking satisfied, Donna grabbed her glass off the nightstand and drained it, giving a delicate shiver after she was done. I wanted to laugh at her obvious distaste for the wine and the fact that she was still drinking it. Unfortunately, I couldn't because I was too twisted up by the point she had just made.

She put her empty glass on the nightstand and leveled her eyes at me. "I can't speak for Lex, Ivie, but I do think that vampire is enamored with you. He watches you when you aren't looking. He wants a taste of you, not just your blood, but all of you."

I couldn't control my mouth. "Yeah, he's had a taste of a lot of women." I pressed my lips together, unable to believe that snide comment came from me.

"Now you're just trying to find a reason not to give him a chance," she said.

I couldn't meet her eyes. I hadn't even told her about my ability to 'call' him to me. Though she probably wouldn't see that as a minus in the relationship department. In fact, I could almost hear her now. *He'd never be able to avoid a conversation. All you'd have to do is make that call and he'd be forced to answer.* She would probably see that as a huge plus.

I shrugged, trying not to seem sullen, even though I was definitely pouting.

Donna's eyes showed her disappointment. "I suppose you were a virgin last night," she said.

I sighed and shook my head. "You're right. That was completely unfair of me. I mentioned that to Lex also this morning, implying that I was one of his harem. He didn't like it."

She was also right about my obvious double standard. When I was younger, I enjoyed experimenting and went through several boyfriends. It wasn't until I hit my mid-twenties that playing it fast and loose lost its appeal. I had no right to sit in judgment of Lex. He had been alive for centuries. Even if he only had one girlfriend every few months or a year, like a human man, he would still have quite a few lovers.

Donna grabbed my hand. "Ivie, I'm not saying that you have to let him Claim you. You don't even have to let him bite you. Just promise me that you won't avoid a relationship just because it's different. There are no guarantees with human men either. The only way you'll know is to try." She took a deep breath. "And don't agree to a Claiming unless you are completely sure that you want to be with Lex for the long haul. It's almost like a marriage between a vampire and a human and it lasts for a minimum of five years. Usually, the human is turned at the end of the five years. It's very rare that a Claiming does not lead to a permanent partnership."

I nodded. "I understand."

Donna got off the bed. "Well, it looks like you're all packed. Wanna see what the boys are doing?"

We walked back downstairs to find Lex and Conner talking in the study.

"Hi, love," Conner said with a smile as we entered the office. "Lex and I are discussing some important Council matters. Do you think you can entertain Ivie for a bit?"

I looked at Lex and found him staring at me. His chocolate brown eyes roamed all over me, possessive and hot.

"No problem. We can find some trouble to get into," Donna answered.

"Will that be ok with you, little one?" Lex asked.

"Sure. We'll get drunk and talk about penises. It'll be fun."

Lex gave me a knowing look and both Conner and Donna laughed. I gave him a little goofy finger wave and followed Donna out of the study and into the kitchen.

As soon as we entered the room, Donna whirled and trapped me against the kitchen counter. "He asked you if you were okay with hanging out for a while. Still think he doesn't see you as an equal partner in the relationship?"

I skirted around her. "Shut up and make me a drink."

She giggled and got to work on getting me drunk.

Chapter Sixteen

[decorative border]

I T WAS DARK before Lex and I left the McMansion. He had to help me up into the SUV because I was pleasantly buzzed and the vehicle was set high off the ground. The ride back to his house was quiet. He seemed to be in a pensive mood and I was contemplating all the things Donna and I had discussed.

He came around the SUV, hauled me out, and we went into the house. Lex grinned at me as I stumbled a little and caught me before I could do any damage to myself.

"Well, there goes my plan for the evening," he murmured.

I smiled slightly. "What?"

He leaned closer and I caught a whiff of his cologne. It was good that his hands were on my hips because my legs went weak. My guard was down because of the strong drinks Donna had mixed for us. Even she had been tipsy when I left and vampires had to drink a lot to feel the effects of alcohol.

"I planned to take you downstairs, put a plug in your ass, and give you so many orgasms that you lost count."

I leaned against him, my legs simply refusing to hold my weight. "Why can't we do that?" I asked.

He chuckled at the wistful tone in my voice. "Because you've had too much to drink. Any time we play, I want you completely sober. It affects your judgment and your ability to determine if something is too much for your body to handle."

I sighed. "Okay."

Lex leaned down and put his mouth to my ear. "That doesn't mean I won't fuck you blind, though."

At his words and the heat of his breath against my temple, my nipples hardened and my clit felt as though it had been zapped with an electrical current.

"Oh my God," I whispered and my legs collapsed completely.

His dark laughter made me shiver as he put one arm behind my back and the other under my knees and lifted me easily. I'd never been with a man who could haul me around like I weighed little more than five pounds.

He moved through the foyer and up the stairs so quickly that my head spun. He reached the bedroom and set me on the bed. I lay back, gasping for breath. All the quick motion made me so dizzy I could barely see.

By the time my head cleared, Lex was standing before me in nothing but a pair of black boxer briefs. I took a deep breath, my balance still off, but not because of the alcohol. He was perfection personified.

As I watched, he pushed the briefs down his legs and kicked them to the side. I hadn't had a chance to really look at him last night. His cock was long, thick, and curved upward slightly. The sight of it made my mouth water.

I started to lean forward and reach toward him, but Lex bent and grabbed the hem of my shirt, whipping it over my head. A few seconds later, he stripped my yoga pants and underwear off my legs. Then he was crawling up from the bottom of the bed and reaching behind me with one hand to unsnap my bra and strip it from me.

My hands flew up to grasp his shoulders. Holy shit, he was moving quickly.

"Lie back," he said, his voice deeper than usual.

I didn't move. I was still trying to process his words when he growled and grabbed my legs, yanking them apart and down. I was flat on my back, staring down the length of my body at him before I could blink.

Lex's dark eyes were painfully bright as they wandered all over my nude body, ending with the area between my thighs. His hands lightly gripped my inner thighs and pressed them wider apart. He growled again, low in his throat.

Normally, the idea of a creature with fangs, growling between my wide-spread thighs, would terrify me. However, I knew exactly what Lex was capable of and I felt heat spreading within me.

I jumped at the first hot swipe of his tongue.

"You taste like candy."

Without my permission my eyes closed and my head fell back as Lex continued to lap at my clit. Suddenly he latched on to the small bundle of nerves with ferocious intent. He was voracious and merciless. In less than a minute, I hung on the edge of the precipice, writhing beneath his mouth.

Too lost in sensation to even form words, I moaned and gasped, hips bucking against his assault. His hard hands pinned me to the mattress.

It was the feeling of him holding me down that threw me over the edge. My back arched so hard only my head touched the mattress and I cried out. The peak was high and sharp enough to cut me in two. The pleasure was so intense it burned like fire throughout my body. Each time I thought it was ending and that I would come down, Lex pushed me higher and harder.

It hurt. Ecstasy and inescapable agony centered on the point between my legs. I screamed, unable to endure it any longer. The blade of my orgasm still sliced through me as Lex lunged upward, thrusting into my body, deep and rough.

He rode me hard. My hands grasped his shoulders, my nails digging into the solid muscle. My eyes drifted shut until one of Lex's hands twisted into my hair and pulled my head back. My chin lifted, leaving my throat exposed.

"Look at me," he demanded, moving faster and harder.

My eyes snapped open and I stared into the deep, dark irises of his. Unbelievably he was building another climax within me, this one promising to be explosive.

"Lex," I whimpered.

I watched as his mouth opened and his canines elongated.

"Lex."

He stared down at me, his face fierce. "Let me in, Ivie. I promise you won't regret it."

Somehow I knew he wasn't just referring to biting me, but also to lowering the barrier surrounding my thoughts.

"Yes," I whispered.

Just as I reached out to him, inviting him into my mind, he struck. I felt his fangs sink into my skin, but it was a delicious pain. At the first pull of his mouth, the tsunami of my orgasm broke over me, breaking down every wall, every defense I erected around my heart and mind. I belonged to him. He owned me, body and soul. And he would for eternity.

Unable to withstand the forces exploding within me, I shrieked. Then my vision went white and there was nothing.

✧   ✧   ✧

I DRIFTED BACK to reality, my senses still raw from the overload. My eyes opened and I looked around. Lex was lying on the bed next to me on his stomach. He had a pillow stuffed under this upper chest and arms and his chin resting on his forearm. His other hand stroked my breast.

When my eyes met his, he grinned and said, "Welcome back."

"Wow."

His grin widened. My head was still fuzzy but my body felt like melted wax.

"I can't move my legs," I mumbled and Lex laughed. I loved making him laugh. The number one reason was because I knew he didn't do it often. However, the fact that his laugh was deep and rich ranked right up there too.

He was still smiling a little when he asked, "Are you okay?"

I nodded. "Is it like that every time you bite during sex?"

The last of his amusement faded from his face. "No. Only with the right person."

My lungs suddenly felt too small. I sucked in a breath. The revelation I'd faced during the peak was in the forefront of my mind, but I couldn't let myself feel it. He didn't want me as I was. He would want to turn me, make me into a vampire as he was. It hurt to know that I wasn't enough.

Still, I played innocent. "What do you mean?"

Lex stared at me, his eyes dark and beautiful just a few inches from my face. He sighed and rolled onto his side.

"I'd hoped to put this conversation off by a bit," he said, running a hand over his face.

Suddenly, I felt very naked and a little anxious. I grabbed the sheet and pulled it over my body, tucking it under my arms. Lex noticed and his mouth tightened, but he didn't say anything.

Instead, he ran a finger up my arm and across my collarbone before his hand cupped my chin and kept me from looking away.

"What we have together is more visceral than anything I have ever experienced," he murmured. "It's special."

I felt a lump forming in my throat. It made my tummy flutter when he said that, yet I also felt as though the walls were closing in on me. I couldn't say anything to stop him, so Lex continued.

"It's rare for vampires and humans to have such a strong connection. When it happens, it's treasured. Conner and Donna had that before he turned her." Lex smiled. "I won't forget how frustrating he found your friend. He couldn't read her mind or control her. It drove him insane for a while." He looked deeply into my eyes. "And you, you can call me. It's a talent very few humans have and, when they do, the vampires of old usually killed them outright. Now, there are a few who remain suspicious of telepaths, but most vampires just try to avoid them."

I felt my eyes getting wider as he continued. Telepath? I wasn't telepathic. Other than this strange ability I had when it came to vampires, I had no other special gifts.

"Conner and I have a theory," he continued.

I blinked at him. A theory? About what? I didn't speak those words out loud, but Lex answered my questions anyway.

"Donna had the ability to erect mental blocks against vampires before she was turned, even the most powerful of us. You have the ability to call me, and probably others of my kind. Conner and I have discussed this. I said that vampire and human connections such as his to Donna and mine to you are rare," he paused, "well, we think that they are signs of our soul mates. That humans meant for vampires are marked with abilities that affect us. Unfortunately, we do not know any others who have met human mates, so we cannot research the hypothesis further."

I barely heard his words after he said 'soul mates'. Soul mates? Even as my soul rejoiced, my mind said I barely knew him. How could we be soul mates? The claustrophobic sensation grew stronger.

"Ivie?" he asked. "Are you okay? You seem agitated."

I didn't speak. All I could do was focus on breathing. Damn right I was agitated. Now it made sense. He pushed so hard for me to move in so he could 'protect' me. He didn't want to protect me. He wanted to control me. My thoughts careened wildly. Did he plan on Claiming me or did he want to turn me whether I agreed or not? Those thoughts, paired with my broken defenses, made me freak right the fuck out.

Unable to remain still, I leapt from the bed and started grabbing my clothes off the floor.

"Ivie?" His voice was full of concern, but slowly edging toward anger.

I couldn't bring myself to care. I was deep in the throes of a gargantuan panic attack.

"Talk to me," he commanded. He did sound a little worried, but now he mostly seemed pissed.

I wiggled into my underwear and yanked my pants up my legs as I spoke. "So what was the plan, Lex? You were going to move me in here, keep me under lock and key until I agreed to a Claiming? Or were you just planning to turn me?"

I didn't bother to look at his face. I was too busy searching for my shirt. I saw it across the room, hanging from the doorknob that led to his closet. In a flash, Lex was in front of me, naked, angry, and as intimidating as hell. I flinched back from him as though he had slapped me. His eyes grew hot and bright, the color of honey in sunlight. I had seen them change before, but not like this.

"What?" he asked, his voice low and menacing. The tone pierced through the veil of panic that surrounded me and I twitched before standing perfectly still.

The look in his eyes reminded me of the tigers in the zoo. Wild and perfectly cold, as though they were just waiting for the right moment to strike and eat your face off.

"Do you think I'm playing some kind of game with you?" he asked, his face inches from mine.

I licked my dry lips. "If it's not a game, what are we doing, Lex? I don't know you, not really. I met you months ago, but the last few days are the most time I've spent with you alone since then. And now you're talking about soul mates and Claiming and special talents."

"And?" he asked. Perhaps he knew where I was going with this or perhaps not, either way, he was going to force me to explain myself.

"I don't want you to turn me," I blurted. To make matters worse, now that I was speaking, I couldn't stop. "I've been trying to avoid you for so long because I know that you think I'm weaker and….less than you, because I am human. I want nothing to do with someone who won't treat me as an equal in the relationship."

"That's not what you were saying a few minutes ago when my cock was between your legs," he roared. "And when in the hell have I ever said that you weren't valuable because you're human?" His face drew closer until I could feel his hot breath on my lips. "I was human before I was turned. It would be a bit hypocritical of me to have that sort of attitude, wouldn't it?"

I watched as he walked to the closet, yanking my shirt off the knob and tossing it to me before he entered. A few seconds later, he reappeared with a pair of jeans in his hands. I watched him slide into them without bothering with underwear.

He was shaking his head as he walked to the dresser against the wall and reached into the top drawer for a t-shirt. I stood with my own shirt clutched to my chest as he pulled his own garment on and then began the process of putting on socks and boots.

The entire time, he was silent and aloof. Finally, he was dressed and stalked across the room to me.

"I did want to Claim you, Ivie, and, yes, eventually turn you. But I wanted to give you time. You have a point. We don't know each other well and you don't have the wisdom and perspective that centuries of living can provide. I was aware of that, so I was willing to wait." His eyes scorched a path from my head to my feet and back again. "Now, I wonder what in the fuck I was thinking?"

He moved around me to the door and I turned to watch him. With a hand on the knob, he turned and looked over his shoulder at me. "Don't worry, my love, I won't force you to be my Claimed and I damn sure won't be turning you. Your precious humanity is safe."

With that horrendously accurate parting shot, Lex opened the bedroom door and left. The door shut behind him with a gentle click. A few moments later I could hear the boom of the front door slamming so hard the entire house seemed to shudder. Which was a feat considering Lex's home was as large, if not larger, than Conner's McMansion.

Shaking, I thrust my arms into my shirt and dragged it over my head. I went downstairs to my bag and fished around for my cell phone. Praying that she wasn't already occupied with Conner, I called Donna.

"Hey, hooker. What did you forget?" she answered breathless and giggling. I could hear the murmur of Conner's voice in the background and knew that I had interrupted them. My chest tightened.

"Hey, Dee. Um, Lex and I had sort of a fight," I whispered. "Can you come get me?"

Despite my determination that it wouldn't happen, tears filled my eyes and began to trickle down my face. Donna, being an incredible friend, didn't hesitate.

"Yes. I'll be there in fifteen minutes. Is Lex still there?"

"No," I said, trying to swallow back the sobs that were threatening to choke me.

"I'll knock when I get there. Have your stuff ready," she said.

"Okay."

I hung up and dashed back upstairs. When I reached the bedroom, I realized that my suitcase was still in the back of Lex's SUV and swore. Well, maybe Conner could get it for me. I didn't think I'd be able to stand seeing Lex again anytime soon.

I went back downstairs and waited by the front door. I paced for what felt like an eternity until I heard a car pull up in the drive. I grabbed my purse and took a deep breath before I opened the door. I didn't want to fall on Donna as a sobbing mess. When I was sure I had myself under control, I threw open the heavy wooden door.

Standing on the other side, baring his teeth, was the vampire that haunted my worst nightmares. I barely managed to scream before he lunged forward and grabbed for me. Just as I had in all my nightmares for the last six months, I turned and ran for my life.

Chapter Seventeen

THE NIGHTMARE WAS BACK. Only this time, I wasn't in the woods. I was in Lex's house, running down a hall. I heard the pounding of feet behind me. Ahead of me was the door that led down to the dungeon. At the bottom of the steps was a heavy steel door, much like the safe room at Conner's house. I knew from what Donna had said to me, that it should be strong enough to keep out a vampire, at least for a while.

I dashed down the stairs. I was three steps from the bottom when I felt fingers brush my shirt. I shrieked and leapt off the stairs, almost diving through the door. I grabbed the door as I went through, slamming it behind me, seeing that face from my nightmare sneering at me just before it shut. I managed to throw the first bolt when he hit the door with a bone-jarring thud.

With shaking hands, I slid home the floor and ceiling bolt. I saw a cross-bar to my left and dropped it in place as well. The heavy door vibrated under the force of his blows, but it held. I suddenly realized how dark it was in the dungeon and ran to the switches on the wall. I turned on every single one, filling the huge space with light. I grabbed the spanking bench and dragged it over to the door, wedging it against the steel to reinforce the locks. I tried to move the St. Andrew's Cross but it was too heavy. I would have to be satisfied with the spanking bench.

Shivering, I looked around the room and realized I was trapped. My purse, which held my phone, was lying on the floor somewhere between the front door and the basement. Unless Lex had a tunnel leading from beneath his house, I was well and truly stuck. I paced through the dungeon, opening the first of the three doors. It was a small but luxurious bathroom. I glanced around, hoping that maybe Lex or the previous owner had been the pretentious sort to have a phone in the bathroom. No such luck. I sighed and exited the bathroom.

I walked to the next door and opened it as well. When I flipped on the switch, I blinked. There were chains and manacles hanging from the corners and some sort of harness set up in the middle of the small room. I assumed it had once been a closet, due to the size. I shivered when I realized what this room might be used for. For punishment or pleasure. When I realized the direction my thoughts had taken, I shook myself out of the daze. Hopefully there would be time for that in the future. If I got out of here alive. And if Lex forgave me.

I decided to throw my pity party later. I had to figure out how to get out of here in one piece before I could begin to worry about fixing things with Lex. I turned off the light to that room and closed the door. I went to the final door on the other wall. I tried to open it, but it was locked. I examined it and couldn't figure out where a key might go.

I stared at the door in confusion for a few minutes before hope began to take hold within me. If the door locked from the other side, perhaps it somehow led to the outside. The bad news was I didn't know how to get out and had no way to call for help.

Suddenly, it hit me that the bangs and thuds at the steel door on the other side of the dungeon had stopped. I crept over to it, trying to be as quiet as possible. I pressed my ear to the metal, trying to hear what might be happening on the other side. At first it was completely silent. I hoped that meant the vampire had given up, but I wasn't about to open the door to find out.

I was just about to give up and go back to the other locked door when I heard something sliding against the steel.

"I can hear you, little rabbit," a deep accented voice said hoarsely.

Every hair on my body stood on end. Holy shit.

Though the door was thick I heard him inhale. "I can smell you too. The fear, gods, it smells divine. I can't wait to fuck that fear out of you before I cut your throat and let your blood spray all over me, then I'll be able to smell it for days."

I jumped away from the door, gagging. I managed to make it to the little bathroom just in time to wretch into the toilet. Oh God, not only was he planning to kill me, the sicko planned to torture me first. I had to find a way out of here.

When I finished dry heaving, I staggered to the sink and rinsed out my mouth before I washed my face with icy cold water. Though I was still scared, the frigid water helped to clear my mind of the unadulterated terror his words had created. As I began to calm, I realized that he should have been able to use mind control on me. Then it became clear, making me feel sick all over again. He wanted to chase me, terrify me, and torture me as long as possible. It was like foreplay for him. I shuddered, scared to death that no one would come for me or that they wouldn't get here in time.

I left the bathroom and headed toward the huge bed in the center of the room. There was nothing I could do at this moment, so I decided to lie on the bed and think. If I could either determine how to unlock the other door and perhaps escape, I might be safe. Or, if I could keep that vampire out long enough, Lex might come home and save me. Still, I couldn't sit around and hope for the best. I needed to do something to help myself because Lex might not return for a long while. Hell, he'd left me for weeks the last time he'd been gone. Granted we hadn't had sex yet, but he was very angry with me. I couldn't risk that he wouldn't return before that vampire got through the steel door.

I turned my face into one of the pillows on the bed. Though I knew the sheets had been changed, since they were now black instead of dark red, I thought I caught a whiff of Lex's scent. I hugged the pillow to me and sniffed deeper, remembering the night I had spent with him in the dungeon and how he had done things to me that I would never forget. Somehow he managed to twine pain and pleasure so completely that they seemed interchangeable. The pain felt incredibly good and the pleasure was so intense that it hurt.

Then I remembered eating dinner with Conner, Donna, and Lex. And cuddling in bed with Lex before going to sleep. He was dry, witty, and, though he didn't laugh often, he made me laugh all the time. He tried to take care of me, both in bed and out of it. In the short time I'd been with Lex, I had fallen hard and fast. I couldn't admit it to him that morning, but I could admit to myself now. All the reasons I tried to avoid him were pointless. I would have avoided the fights and ugliness if I'd had the courage to talk to him about what I was thinking and feeling.

I was in love with a vampire. The thought was both terrifying and exhilarating. Not that it mattered if I couldn't get the hell out of this room.

I was thinking so intently about Lex that I could almost hear his voice and smell his skin. Then it hit me, I had called Lex before. Maybe I could call him again. Get him to come to me and bring help. The only problem was that I didn't know how I did it. I was asleep the first time and hadn't bothered to try again because it freaked me out so badly.

Now, I needed him. I lay back on the bed, staring at the ceiling, and focused on Lex. I tried to relax and open my mind. Deep within me something clicked into place. I felt something tug from the vicinity of my heart.

Lex?

I didn't say it out loud because I knew that, if the vampire was still at the door, he would be able to hear me.

I didn't get an answer, though I did feel that tug again.

Can you hear me?

The sensation in my abdomen intensified.

I need your help. The vampire that kidnapped me before is at your house. I'm locked in the basement, but I think he's going to find a way in.

There was nothing for a moment, then emotion bombarded me so hard and fast that I couldn't differentiate them. I gasped and sat straight up on the bed. My heart felt like it was going to explode as I choked and coughed, trying to deal with the flood of thoughts and emotions that swamped me.

Just as quickly as it arrived, the explosion was cut off. I still felt that connection but I was no longer overwhelmed. I was about to reach out to Lex again when I heard clanging at the steel door to the basement. I watched in horror as sparks began to shoot from around the edge of the door.

I jumped to my feet and ran over to the door. I placed a hand on the metal and jerked it away. It was hot. Shit, I wasn't positive, but I had a bad feeling they were cutting through the door with a torch.

Lex, hurry.

There was no response. Since it sounded as though they were going to get through the door before Lex arrived, I decided it was time to be honest with him and myself.

I'm so sorry about the things I said. I overreacted. I was stupid. I should have just talked to you about how I was feeling.

Again there was no response.

In case I don't see you again, I just wanted to say that... I love you.

The tugging sensation in my abdomen turned into a tightening. The sensation was strange, almost comforting. I heard low voices talking and then more metal banging then curses from whoever was trying to break through the door. I thought I heard a low howl over the noise.

Everything went silent. My heart started pounding harder. Another howl, closer this time. Then another. And another. It sounded like an entire pack of wolves had invaded Lex's house. I didn't move, didn't even breathe.

Suddenly there was a flurry of activity on the other side of the door. I heard feet pounding on the stairs. I wanted so badly to throw open the door and make a run for it, but I stayed put. I didn't know if those were real wolves or werewolves. Donna had mentioned something about werewolves not long ago, but I never had a chance to ask her for more details.

A hand closed over my shoulder and I screamed, wheeling around and throwing myself back against the steel door. When I saw Lex standing in front of me, his hands up as though in surrender, I cried out again and dove at him. I wrapped my arms around his torso and burrowed in, glad to no longer be alone and, hopefully, safe.

"Thank God you came," I gasped.

Lex's arms closed around me so tight I could barely breathe. I didn't say a single word though. I just needed him to hold me until my teeth stopped chattering.

Lex pulled away, removing my arms from his waist. That stung, but I understood. It was over. He didn't want me after the terrible things I said to him before, even if I had apologized. I couldn't blame him.

"We need to get out of here while they're distracted," he murmured, ushering me across the dungeon and to the door that had been locked until just a few minutes ago.

I couldn't keep up because my legs were weak from the relief of someone coming to save me. Lex stopped and scooped me up in his arms, striding through the door. He closed it behind him and locked it with one hand, then headed down a hallway so dark that I couldn't see anything. Grateful for his excellent night vision, I looped my arms around his neck and closed my eyes.

A few moments later, he kicked open another door and carried me out into the bright sunlight. I hissed and shut my eyes again. I heard the tires of a car screech to a halt nearby. When I cracked open my eyelids, I saw Conner's SUV. Lex carried me to the rear door, opened it, and set me inside. He gently pushed me over and climbed in next to me.

I looked up and saw Conner in the driver's seat and Finn in the passenger side. They both looked at me, anger and relief warring in their expressions.

"Is she okay?" Finn asked.

"Yes," Lex answered tightly.

Okay, Lex was still mad about the whole Finn thing. Good to know. I felt hot breath on my neck a second before a long, wet tongue slid from my jaw line up to my temple. I jerked my head away and twisted around. A freaking wolf was in the back of the SUV, his head stuck over the backseat, panting in my face.

He started to lick me again when Lex's hand appeared and shoved the wolf's snout away. The animal snarled and snapped at him.

"Goddammit, Calder, keep your fucking tongue off my woman. I don't want her to get fleas."

I watched as the wolf began to change before my very eyes. The fur receded in a wave, leaving only smooth, tan skin. I heard bones cracking as they shifted within flesh. I winced because it sounded extremely painful. A few moments later, I was staring at an exceptionally beautiful man. His hair was golden brown, like caramel, and his eyes were green with a starburst of amber around his pupil. His light brown skin was stretched taut over lean, cut muscle. And he was completely naked.

I closed my eyes and turned to face the front seat again. Holy shit, I just saw a strange man's, er, werewolf's penis. And it was just as gorgeous as the rest of him.

"Christ, Calder, cover yourself. You're going to traumatize her more than she already is!" Lex exclaimed.

Calder chuckled. "Judging by the way her heart is racing and she's blushing, I don't think she's traumatized. Maybe she's wishing yours was as nice."

I made an outraged sound and heard the thud of flesh hitting flesh.

"Ow! No need for violence, Alexander. I was only teasing the girl. You know I'm partial to bitches in heat."

I threw a scowl over my shoulder at the werewolf called Calder. He now had a shirt covering his lap, but he looked unrepentant.

Lex chuckled. "He's being quite literal, little one. He prefers she-wolves of his pack and only when they are in the mating heat."

I rolled my eyes.

"Human women are so….fragile," Calder said playfully. "I want a woman I don't have to worry about breaking when I fuck her."

"Shut up, wolf, before I muzzle you," Lex growled.

Calder snarled back but didn't say anything else.

The insanity of the last few hours overwhelmed me. That was the only reason that I decided their bickering was hysterically funny. I started to laugh and laugh. I couldn't stop. I was laughing so hard that tears were streaming down my face. Then I was no longer laughing but sobbing uncontrollably.

Lex gathered me in his arms, tucking my head under his chin. "I have you, little one. Let it all out."

I closed my eyes and leaned against him. He stroked my hair and my back, his petting calming me. Finally, the tears slowed and I hiccupped a few times.

My eyelids felt heavy, the prolonged stress and fear taking their toll on me.

"It's okay, Ivie. Go to sleep. I'll be here when you wake up."

I snuggled closer into Lex's chest, inhaling his scent. Then I let myself pretend that he would hold me forever as I drifted to sleep. I wished for it so hard, that I dreamed of it even in my slumber.

Chapter Eighteen

A HAND CUPPED my shoulder, shaking me gently.

"Ivie? Wake up, little one. We're here."

I opened my eyes and blinked up at Lex's implacable face. He was standing in the open door on the passenger side of the nondescript sedan that had been waiting for us at Conner's house. Lex had woken me just enough to usher me into the passenger seat of the sedan before we were off again.

I wasn't sure how long I had been asleep, but it had to have been hours because it was dark outside. I let Lex help me sit up and climb out of the car.

I yawned. "Where are we?"

"Safe house," he answered shortly. "I can't tell you where."

I nodded tiredly. He couldn't tell me because I was human and thus vulnerable to vampire telepathy, I got it. Honestly, after the day I had, I didn't want to know anyway. The house was actually more of a cabin in the middle of nowhere. The night air was cooler than usual and I wondered how far north we had gone.

I shivered as he led me to the front door. I realized that he wasn't even attempting to carry me as he had before. It made me feel even colder. Obviously, he couldn't forgive me.

I followed him into the dark house. As soon as the door was shut behind us, he turned on the lights to reveal a simple interior that held a few comfortable furnishings. The living, dining, and kitchen areas were all open to one another. Rustic, braided rugs covered wood floors and a huge fireplace dominated the corner to the right of the front door and the kitchen was to the left side of the room. A short hallway was directly across from the front door but I could see three other doors.

I realized that I was extremely thirsty as well as exhausted, so I staggered into the kitchen and opened cabinets until I found glasses. I filled it directly from the tap in the sink and drained the glass. Lex was standing a few feet away, watching me.

"Let me show you where the bedroom is and you can clean up while I get our things."

His words didn't completely penetrate the fog around my brain, but I nodded. I followed him down the hall. He opened the second door on the right and I saw a king-size bed in the middle of the room.

"The bathroom is the door across the hall if you want to take a shower," he said.

I nodded and turned to find it. I was so tired but I needed a shower. The cold sweat of fear did not smell great a few hours later. I went into the bathroom and flipped on the light. I gaped at the enormous claw-foot tub standing in the middle of the room.

I decided that I wasn't too tired for a bath and set about filling the tub with hot water and added some bath salts I found sitting on a shelf next to the tub. While the water ran, I stripped my clothes off, leaving them in a pile by the door. A quick search of the drawers and cabinets yielded a towel, washcloth, and hair band. I bundled my hair on top of my head, set the towel and cloth on a little table conveniently located next to the tub.

I found some shower gel next to the bath salts and put it on the table with my towel. Finally, the tub was half full, so I turned off the faucet and slid into the water. It was so hot that I gasped slightly but I didn't care. I settled into the tub, leaning against the curved back. Within minutes, my muscles were relaxing and I felt less strung out.

After I almost dozed off for the second time, I decided to finish up and get into bed. I took the washcloth and dunked it in the water. I added shower gel and quickly soaped and rinsed my skin. The soothing lavender and vanilla scent relaxed me enough that I hoped I wouldn't have nightmares.

I climbed out, dried off, and wrapped the towel around me. The air in the cabin was cool against my damp skin, but I didn't care. I just wanted a bed and some sleep. I pulled the plug in the tub and took the time to rinse it out. It wasn't my house and I didn't want to leave a mess for someone else to clean up.

I took my hair down and used the comb I'd found in one of the drawers. With a sigh, I tightened the towel around me and hoped that I could at least find a man's shirt or something to sleep in. I left the bathroom and went into the bedroom Lex had shown me. I almost moaned in relief when I saw my suitcase sitting on the bed. I didn't care how it got there, but I was just glad to have it.

I unzipped it and threw back the lid. All my clothes and toiletries were still inside. I grabbed a shirt I liked to sleep in, a pair of panties, and my deodorant. I put on my underwear, used my deodorant, and yanked the shirt over my head. I grabbed my suitcase and set it on the chair next to the bed.

Still chilled, I pulled the quilts down, settled down into the mattress, and wrapped the blankets over me, doing my best to make myself into a blanket burrito. Without bothering to turn out the lamp, I dropped like a stone into a deep, dreamless sleep.

I was so out of it that Lex came into the room, stripped off his clothes, and stretched out next to me and I never even moved.

As he wrapped his arms around me and tucked me against his side, I also had no idea that I murmured the words, "Love you," in my sleep.

❖ ❖ ❖

THE NEXT MORNING, I woke up surrounded by heat. Arms held me tight and close to a hard, naked chest. Lex's thigh pinned my legs to the mattress. He was wrapped around me like a boa constrictor. I blinked in the dim light of the bedroom. My cheek was smashed against Lex's pectoral. I desperately needed the bathroom. I tried to roll over but his arms tightened even further, keeping me in place.

I tried to speak, but all that came out was a croak. I cleared my throat. "Lex," I rasped, "I need to get up."

His arms relaxed and I rolled out of bed. When my feet hit the cold boards on the floor, I gasped. Now that I was no longer under the blankets and wrapped up in Lex's arms, I realized that the room was very chilly.

I dashed to the bathroom, hearing Lex's quiet chuckle behind me. The toilet seat was ice cold, so I hurried through the entire process. The water that came out of the tap when I washed my hands was even colder.

I ran back into the bedroom and dove under the blankets. My relationship, if you could call it that, with Lex might be over, or at least on its last legs, but I figured he wouldn't mind me snuggling up to him since he'd been wrapped around me before. I slid across the big bed until I was touching him from shoulder to knee. My feet were freezing from my quick trip to the bathroom, so I stuck them against Lex's calves. He jumped.

"You're feet are like ice," he grumbled, still half asleep, but he cuddled me closer.

Shivering, I tucked my cold nose against his ribs, making him jump again. "Doesn't this place have heat?" I asked, teeth chattering.

"Only the fireplace in the front room and a gas heater in the bathroom. I forgot to turn it on last night."

Great. I could have been saved the frostbite on my ass cheeks. I didn't say anything, though. I figured saving said ass from the bad guys earned Lex a break from nagging for at least five or ten years. Though I probably wouldn't see much of him unless he was at Conner and Donna's.

I tilted my head back to look up into his sleepy, sexy face. "Thank you for coming to get me."

He squeezed me tighter. "I will always come for you," he answered.

I stared at him in confusion. "But, I thought…" I trailed off as he scowled at me.

"I know what you thought. I felt everything you felt yesterday when you called to me. And that's not what's happening between us."

I bit my lip. "Okay." I took a deep breath. "I am sorry about, you know, before."

Lex's face softened and his hand cupped my cheek. "I'm sorry too, little one. I shouldn't have left you alone." He kissed me. "You also need to talk to me about what you're feeling and thinking. Though I can read your mind, I promised I wouldn't."

"You're right." I was ashamed of my behavior. I had always been so good at communicating with my boyfriends, but I seemed to have forgotten how with Lex. I put a hand on his chest, holding back a giggle when he flinched from my cold fingers. "So, what is happening with us?" I asked.

Lex buried his fingers in my hair, massaging my scalp gently. "How about you tell me what you want, then I'll tell you what I want, and, if we need to, we determine a compromise?"

I stared at his gorgeous brown eyes for a moment before I nodded. He smiled slightly and waited. I realized he wanted to have this conversation at this moment. Crap.

"I'm going to be honest, Lex. I'm not sure exactly what I want for us. I do know that I don't want to jump into anything too quickly, but I also want to see you and spend time with you. I don't want a life without you." I paused. "It's just, to be with you, I feel this unspoken expectation that I'll have to change *everything* if I want to keep you and I'm not ready to make such an irrevocable commitment."

Lex watched me, his expression tender. His stroking fingers tugged lightly as he combed them through my hair.

"This is what I want," he said. Then…nothing.

I waited before I asked, "And?"

He grinned. "This. You and me. Together. Nothing else matters to me."

My breath backed up in my chest. Holy cow.

He continued to blow my mind. "I know you love me and want to be with me. I also want you to know that I love you and I will take you however I can get you." He stopped, letting me digest his words. Before I could finish, he went on, his face turning serious. "Will I want to turn you eventually? Yes, but I can give you time, years if I have to. I want you to be ready before we take a step we can't take back. I know what I want for myself, but I want you to be certain of your feelings before you change your entire future."

I was seconds away from hyperventilating because my breathing was so fast. "What do you want for yourself?" I asked, unable to stop the question from tumbling out of my mouth.

"To be with you forever."

Those unabashedly romantic words from such a big, intimidating man made tears fill my eyes.

"How can you know that?" I asked. "We've only known each other a few months, and mostly in passing."

Lex smiled at me again. "I have lived so many lifetimes, little one. I have made mistakes. In that time, I've also learned a great deal. Most importantly, I have learned how to recognize what I want. I knew, the first moment I saw you and spoke to you and heard the thoughts that you used to project so loudly, that you were mine."

While part of me wanted to swoon at his words, the twenty-first century woman raised her eyebrows, "Yours?"

He chuckled. "Yes, you are mine. You belong to me." He kissed me lightly, even though I was trying to pull away a little. "And I am yours. Everything I am belongs to you."

I loved hearing that from him. The swoon that threatened at his previous words came back full force. In order to cover how touched I was at his words, I quipped, "Well, I guess it's okay as long as it goes both ways."

Lex's face grew serious. "There are things we need to talk about, Ivie, about what's going on amongst the vampires. You need to know what we're facing."

For the first time, Lex wasn't excluding me because I was human. He was finally going to tell me what was going on.

"You don't think that it's too dangerous to tell me?"

He shook his head. "They came for you even though you knew nothing. I know the way Cornelius works and he would know that we didn't share information with you. He sent his men anyway."

The small bloom of hope in my chest withered. Okay, so he still viewed me as weak. Even though he said he loved me and that he would give me time, it still stung.

"Tell me what you're thinking, little one."

My eyes jumped back to his. "Nothing. Just wondering what they wanted me for since I would be pretty worthless to them."

Lex was back to scowling. "Worthless? I don't believe that's what you were thinking, though we will be discussing your word choices in a little while. Now, I want you to tell me the truth, and do not forget what I said I would do to you if you lied to me."

I sighed. While our play had been fun, I was a little afraid to see what Lex would do to me if I pushed him.

"Sometimes, I feel like you see me as weaker, well, less valuable than you because I'm human," I murmured. "You don't tell me things and you try to keep me under lock and key. It, um, makes me think that you see me as inadequate."

His expression was thunderous. "That is not what I'm doing at all. I want to protect you. Your safety is more valuable to me than my own. I withhold information because it will keep you safe."

I narrowed my eyes at him. Did he seriously believe that bullshit? It hit me then that, for all his smooth, urbane appearance, Lex was a man born almost a thousand years ago. He didn't think the way a 21st century guy would. In fact, his attitudes were very progressive for a man of his era, but still archaic by modern standards.

I sighed. It looked like I would have to educate him. Something told me that a man alive for nearly a millennia would be more difficult to train than any twenty or thirty-something year old guy I'd dated in the last few years.

"Lex," I said in order to get his attention. "I'm going to tell you something that will make your life easier when it comes to me."

His eyebrows lifted but he didn't say anything.

I took this as an invitation to continue. "I don't see your silence as protection, Lex. I see it as you not considering me an equal in our relationship. Women of my generation expect equal partnership."

Lex stared at me for a moment before he threw his head back and laughed. He roared with laughter until I started to get irritated. I poked him in the ribs.

"Hey, I'm being serious. Laughing at me is not the best way to get on my good side."

He stopped chuckling long enough to kiss me. "I'm sorry, little one. You are very funny. Of course I see you as an equal in our relationship. Why wouldn't I?"

I pouted a bit. "Well, you are close to a thousand years old. I thought maybe your thoughts on women were a bit antiquated."

Lex grinned and I could see he was trying not to laugh. "Ivie, in the vampire culture, women are just as dangerous and powerful as men. While the general attitude of most vampires my age is that women do not have as much power as the men, they know better. They may not admit it, but to forget that fact would lead to their death much earlier than they would like." He grew serious. "Still, you have to understand that I will do whatever it takes to keep you safe, even if it means keeping you in the dark about certain things. I would do the same for Conner or Finn."

Before I had a chance to argue, he rolled us both out of bed and smacked me playfully on the ass.

"Now, I'm going to get a fire started while you get dressed and make us some coffee."

As he left the room, I rubbed my ass cheek and decided not to point out how sexist his directive was in case he decided to spank me again.

Chapter Nineteen

꜖꜖꜖꜖꜖꜖꜖꜖꜖꜖꜖꜖꜖꜖꜖꜖꜖꜖꜖꜖꜖꜖꜖꜖꜖꜖꜖꜖꜖꜖꜖꜖

SINCE LEX HAD yanked me out of bed against my will, I considered ignoring his directives and just climbing back into the warm bed. I realized quickly that this was probably not the best idea, so I threw on a pair of comfy plaid pajama pants that I found in my suitcase. I also pulled on a pair of socks to protect my feet from the cold floor. When I went into the bathroom to wash my face and brush my teeth, I noticed that Lex had turned on the heater in the bathroom.

After I finished my morning routine, I walked down the hall and heard the merry crackling of a fire. I saw that a pile of firewood had been brought in and sat to the side of the hearth. The front door was slightly ajar and Lex was nowhere in sight. I assumed he was getting more firewood.

I went into the kitchen and started digging around in the cabinets until I found coffee. As I looked around, I realized I had coffee but no coffee maker. I opened several cabinet doors before I gave up.

The front door swung open and I turned to see Lex coming through the door with another stack of firewood in his arms. He kicked the door shut behind him and went to put the wood down by the fireplace.

"Um, Lex?"

"Yes?" He wasn't looking at me as he threw another small log on the fire.

"Where's the coffeemaker?"

He glanced up at me then. "What?"

I lifted the canister of coffee and shook it. "I have coffee but no coffeemaker."

Like any other man I'd ever met, he immediately came into the kitchen and started opening cabinets, searching for the machine. I sighed and set the can down on the counter top. I watched as he did exactly what I had just done. Which meant he opened every door and looked on every shelf.

After a few moments, he pulled out a weird carafe that I recognized as a French press. I hadn't even noticed it.

"I think this is our only option," he said, setting the press next to the stove.

I stared at it. Though I knew what it was, I'd never used one before. "I have no idea how that works," I said.

Lex chuckled. "Then I guess I'll do the fire and the coffee."

I nodded and went to the fridge to see if there was anything I could make for breakfast. I didn't hold a great deal of affection for the process of cooking but I could at least make some eggs and maybe some toast. I found the fridge stocked with the basics; eggs, cheese, milk, butter, and deli meat. There was small jar of mayonnaise and a container of mustard also.

I grabbed eggs and cheese and figured I could throw together some scrambled eggs. I was pretty sure there would be bread somewhere in the kitchen, so I would make toast to go with it. While Lex put water in a small pot to boil for coffee, I started the process of making breakfast.

As I broke eggs into a bowl, I glanced at him.

"Can I ask where we are?"

Lex faced me with surprise on his face. "What?"

I started beating eggs with a fork. "Well, last night, you wouldn't tell me where we are, and this morning you said you would let me in on what's happening. So, the first thing I want to know is, where are we?"

He looked at me with the strangest expression on his face. "Okay. We're about five miles south of the Oklahoma-Kansas border, north of Bartlesville."

I nodded even though I had no idea where Bartlesville, Oklahoma was. Though now I understood why it was so cool here. It was late October and we were much further north than Dallas. Lex grinned at me as though he understood exactly what I was thinking.

"What else do you want to know?" he asked.

I seasoned the eggs and poured them into the warm pan. I began to stir them with a spatula as I thought about what I wanted to know. Honestly, I wanted to learn everything.

I decided to start with the immediate issues first and go from there.

"Why did that vampire come after me and who is he? I thought you said he was dead."

Lex took the pot off the stove and poured the boiling water over the coffee grounds.

"The man you saw yesterday is Claus Hoffmann. He isn't the vampire that kidnapped you with Donna. That was his twin brother, Johann. Johann is dead. I know it for a fact because I killed him myself."

The shiver that went up my spine at his words had nothing to do with the cool temperatures and everything to do with the icy rage in his voice.

"Finn and Conner explained about The Faction, correct?"

I shrugged. "A little. They didn't go into a lot of detail."

"Well, originally, we thought they merely wanted vampires to reveal themselves and reign over humans in some sort of twisted monarchy. While that is a major part of the plan, there is more. They not only want to control humans, they want to rid the world of mixed-blood vampires."

I really didn't understand that. "What?"

Lex began the process of filtering the grounds out of the liquid before he answered me. I didn't push because I could tell he was gathering his thoughts.

"Mixed-blood vampires are those who were turned. Some vampires can be born, but most couples try for decades before that happens. Something about the differences in our blood make it more difficult for the females to get pregnant. Our species would have died out long ago if we hadn't begun to turn humans."

I would have to ponder that later. Basically, he just told me that humans not only served as food for vampires but also saved their species by turning.

"If The Faction has their way, then Conner, Finn, and I will all be killed. Only Asher would remain because he was born a vampire."

I had only met Asher in passing a few months before, but that was something I had not known.

Lex grabbed two mugs out of the top cabinet and poured coffee into them as he continued to speak. "And I am almost certain that any pure bloods that oppose these changes will be taken out of the equation as well."

I accepted the coffee cup he handed. "So you're talking about vampire genocide perpetrated by other vampires? That sounds a little far-fetched," I said. "I mean, why would they want to do that?"

Lex leaned a hip against the counter opposite me. "Why would anyone want to elevate a certain group of people? Hitler, for example. Part of his policies were pure madness, but, really, his main motivation was the accumulation of power. Cornelius wants power. Not just over humans, but the entire world."

I honestly didn't understand why anyone would want that kind of headache. I mean, it sounded like the goal of a villain in an Austin Powers movie. Sure, it sounded like a sexy job title, but the actual work would be a pain in the ass.

He distracted me from my internal tangent by speaking again. "There are quite a few natural born vampires that share Cornelius' feelings."

I sipped my coffee, surprised that Lex had added just the right amount of sugar and milk. "But vampires aren't immortal, right? And humans outnumber you. What's to stop them from ganging up on The Faction and taking them out?"

Lex nodded. "That's a fair question and a smart one. We aren't sure what Cornelius intends to do to prevent those actions from humans, but there has to be some sort of plan in place."

"Well, I still don't understand how I play into it," I said.

Lex sipped his coffee and appeared to be contemplating my comment. "The most logical reason would be to use you as leverage against me. Claus is eager for revenge over the death of his twin and Cornelius wants to further his agenda amongst our kind."

Holy shit. This Claus guy wanted to kidnap me as part of his revenge against Lex. Considering the things his brother had threatened to do to me, I was scared shitless about what he might do in order to punish Lex. I had to set my cup on the counter because my hand began to shake.

To put it in words that Donna used on a regular basis, shit just got very real.

✧   ✧   ✧

AFTER I FINISHED making our breakfast, I asked Lex a few more questions about the current situation and vampire history. He was an excellent teacher. I mentioned this to him, and he said that he usually taught vampire history to those who wanted to be turned.

I was pleasantly surprised when he helped clean up the kitchen after we ate. I mentioned this to him, which made him laugh.

"Little one, I've been alive for hundreds of years. The first few decades after I was turned, I took care of myself because I didn't want to risk the staff discovering what I am. I know how to cook, wash dishes, even wash clothes. The only reason I have a house-keeper now is due to my duties as a Council member and running my nightclubs. Though I would prefer to have my privacy, I do not have the time to do those things for myself any longer."

I was shocked by his words. Most of the men I knew couldn't remember to put their dirty socks in the laundry hamper, much less use a washing machine. And forget about cooking and doing the dishes. They left that to their wives. I found it amazing that Conner and Lex were so domesticated considering the eras they were born. Women were little better than slaves during their time as humans.

Maybe I had misunderstood Lex's thoughts on our relationship more than I realized. By his behavior the last few hours, he did value me and see me as a partner rather than a possession. Several of the things he did that upset me were done out of a desire to protect me from harm rather than viewing me as weak. I really was an idiot for not talking to him about my concerns earlier.

Once the kitchen was tidied, I followed Lex into the living area and settled on a chair near the fireplace as he added more wood to the fire.

"So what now?" I asked.

After he threw the last log on the blaze, he stood and brushed his hands together. "We need to stay here for a few days until the security at my home is tested and updated. The specialists Conner and I hired aren't sure how they got through the gate without setting off the alarms or ringing the house. It shouldn't have been possible for them to get so close to the house without alerting you or the security firm I hired."

I nodded. "What are we supposed to do for the next two or three days then?"

The expression on Lex's face became deliciously wicked.

"We play."

I swallowed hard as heat rushed through my body. Even dressed in a plain black t-shirt and broken-in, faded jeans, Lex projected power and sophistication. I started to stand from my chair, but he shook his head.

"Stay there. Do not move unless I tell you. Do you remember what to call me?"

I nodded.

Lex's brow furrowed and he growled, "That's five."

"Sorry?" I asked.

"That's another three. I just reminded you how to address me, Ivie." His voice was stern.

Shit. "I'm sorry, Sir."

He nodded. "I would say you get another five for insincerity, but I think eight will be enough to gain an honest apology for being disrespectful. Do you remember your safe word?"

"Zebra, Sir."

I started to ask him what he was talking about, but remembered just in time that I wasn't supposed to speak unless he asked me a direct question or to say my safe word. I swallowed hard again and watched as he moved the coffee table off the huge braided rug that was surrounded by the sofa and two chairs. Then he walked to the armchair opposite of me and sat down, crossing his leg so that his right ankle rested on his left knee.

"Strip and get on your hands and knees, facing away from me," he commanded.

Now that the fire was burning brightly, the room was much warmer, but, still, I shivered. Without rushing, I stood and removed my shirt and bra, followed by my pants, undies, and socks. When I turned to get on my hands and knees, my back to him, I hesitated.

"Now, Ivie," he stated.

I bit my lip and lowered myself down onto the rug, getting into position. I felt extremely vulnerable and exposed.

"Spread your knees further apart."

I moved my legs another couple of inches. Suddenly, his hand gave my inner thigh a light, but still stinging, slap.

"More."

I sucked in a deep breath and spread my legs another six inches apart, feeling more naked than I'd ever felt in my life.

"Better," he said approvingly. "Now, arch your back and tilt your ass up in the air."

This time I didn't hesitate to do as he said because my inner thigh was still burning slightly from the slap he'd given me. Though I had to admit to myself that it had woken up the nerve endings in the lower half of my body.

"Perfect," he murmured. "So pretty and pink."

I realized he was talking about my pussy and I was certain my entire body was blushing. He could see *everything*.

"And you're already wet for me," he continued. "That's beautiful." He paused. "Have you ever been fucked in the ass, Ivie?"

I shook my head vehemently as I said, "No, Sir."

"Is it something you would like to try?" he asked.

I grew very still. I wasn't sure I wanted to do something like that, but knew a lot of women enjoyed it.

"Ivie?" Lex's voice was gentle, prompting.

"I-I don't know, Sir," I answered.

He hummed. "Well, we may start small and you can decide from there."

I wanted to ask him what the hell that meant because he was freaking me out, but I was distracted by the sound of his belt buckle jingling and the hiss of leather as he removed the belt from the loops of his jeans. I hadn't realized that he stood.

He draped the belt over my waist and I almost jumped at the cool touch of the leather. Then I heard the rasp of his zipper and the rustle of fabric as he pushed his jeans down his legs. There was more movement and a whisper of fabric hitting the leather of the armchair. Even though I couldn't see him, I knew Lex was naked.

"Now, I believe you earned eight lashes for forgetting to be respectful and an insincere apology. Am I correct?"

I lowered my head as I realized that was why he draped the belt over my waist. "Yes, Sir," I whispered.

"I want you to count them out loud. You do not have to thank me, but I do expect you to apologize again when we're done and mean it."

"Yes, Sir."

Lex removed the belt from my waist and I heard him snap the leather together. It was a menacing sound.

The first blow stung more than when he had spanked me with his hand. A lot more.

"One," I gasped.

The second wasn't quite as bad and on the other cheek. "Two."

I barely finished the word when the belt landed across both of my ass cheeks, but it was a little harsher than the one before. While the pain was at the forefront, I still felt a little curl of heat in my belly as my skin stung.

"Three."

He paused for a moment, letting the burn of the lashes fade slightly. The next blow was lower on my right cheek, nearer to my thigh.

"Four." My voice was tight as I spoke. He repeated the blow on the other side. "Five."

I counted six and seven as he landed the belt across the middle of both cheeks in quick succession, stealing my breath. I felt him drop to his knees.

"Last one, Ivie. This one will sting. Are you ready?"

"Yes, Sir."

Suddenly, the belt slapped between my spread legs, falling dead center of my clit and labia. I gasped, my back arching further, and hips bucking against the burning sensation. I vaguely heard the belt clatter to the floor before Lex thrust his thumb inside of me.

"Fuck, you're soaked," he growled. He pressed downward, against the front wall of my vagina and my hips bucked again. "Apologize for your disrespectful behavior, Ivie."

I whimpered. "I'm sorry, Sir. Please forgive me."

He moved behind me, his knees outside of mine, caging me in. His thumb disappeared and I felt the head of his cock pressing against me. With one smooth motion, he thrust into me. I moaned and felt my internal muscles clench from the sensation of suddenly being full.

"Apology accepted," he groaned.

His thumb moved up from where he was deep inside me to brush across the rosette of my asshole. I froze, alien sensations bombarding me. No one had ever touched me there before during sex. I was shocked at how intense the small touch felt.

"Rub your clit, Ivie, while I fuck you," he instructed as he began to move his hips, pulling out and pressing his cock deeper with each thrust. Each time, his thumb would lightly press into my ass.

I moved my hand between my legs, my fingers finding my wet and swollen clit. As I drew closer to the peak, Lex moved his thumb against my ass each time he thrust into me. I continued to touch myself, my orgasm bearing down on me like a freight train at maximum speed because of his dual assault on my body. My breath came in pants and my thighs trembled. Finally, he pressed his thumb inside me. The intensity created as he breached me for the first time threw me over the edge.

I threw my head back and cried out as my body clamped down on his cock and his thumb. The orgasm seemed to last forever. Lex timed his strokes so that his dick and thumb were in perfect sync, wringing every last ounce of pleasure from me that he could.

"Fuck, that's perfect," he groaned as his thrusts became jerky and I knew he was coming with me.

Unable to hold myself upright any longer, my arms collapsed and I crumpled face first on the rug. Lex gently removed his thumb from my ass and braced himself over me with both hands, breathing hard.

After a few moments, I whimpered as he pulled his dick from my body, but didn't move. I heard him walk into the kitchen area and turn the water on. He washed his hands and opened and closed a drawer. A few moments later he came back with a damp cloth.

"Spread your legs," he said softly.

I did as he asked, still sprawled on my stomach as he cleaned me. I heard him walk away again. He returned to stretch out on the rug next to me, throwing his thigh over mine and pressing his chest against my back. I sighed in contentment as he ran his fingers through my hair, not even minding the hard floor beneath me.

"I need to put salve on your skin, little one," he murmured.

"Later, please," I said. "I like the way you're holding me now."

His lips touched my shoulder. "All right, Ivie."

Somewhere in the house I heard his cell phone ringing.

"Dammit," he whispered.

"Don't answer it."

With a sigh, he rolled away and got to his feet. "I have to. I'm waiting on a call from Conner."

He padded down the hall on bare feet. I let myself drift on a cloud of relaxation. I heard him speaking quietly for a few moments then return to the living room.

"Ivie, you need to get up and get dressed. We have to go back to the city."

I rolled onto my back and the look on his face had me jerking upright.

"What happened?" I asked.

Lex's jaw was hard, his eyes burning with black fire. "The Faction took your friends."

"Who?" I shot to my feet.

"All of them. Ricki, Kerry, and Shannon."

Fear took over my body as I began to throw on my clothes. Then, I did something I'd rarely done before. I prayed.

Chapter Twenty

THE NEXT FIVE HOURS were some of the worst of my life. Lex repacked my bag for me, since I was too much of a basket case to finish. Then he ushered me into the car and we took off. The sedan was older and sort of a junker. Lex pushed it, trying to get every bit of power out of the engine, but top speed was ninety. We were pulled over twice, but Lex used his vampire mojo to get us on our way.

It was mid-afternoon by the time we made it back to Dallas. Lex drove us straight to Conner's house. After he rang the bell at the gate and we were on our way down the drive, I saw several cars out in front of the house. Probably close to ten. It hit me then that Conner, Lex, and their brethren were going all out to get my friends back and my eyes filled with tears.

Lex parked and turned off the car. I used a tissue from my purse to wipe my eyes as he came around the car as I climbed out. He took my hand as we walked up to the front door. After Lex pressed the doorbell, Finn answered the door, looking both pissed and tired.

Lex stiffened next to me but relaxed quickly. They nodded to one another is some silent show of camaraderie. Finn stepped back and we entered the house.

"Donna and Conner are in the ballroom, talking to the others," Finn said.

After a quick stop to the bathroom to relieve myself and wash my face, I went into the ballroom. I stopped short when I saw that the room was a hive of activity. There were probably close to fifty people in there. Some I knew were vampires. I also saw the werewolf, Calder, with a group of men and women that I assumed were part of his pack. He nodded to me and I lifted my chin back.

I saw Donna talking with Conner and Lex and headed their way. A woman suddenly stepped in front of me, her eyes narrowing on me with unconcealed hunger. She had long black hair, golden skin, and gorgeous eyes the color of honey. Even I had to admit she was incredibly regal and beautiful and I was definitely not interested in women.

Oh shit. There was no time for this.

"Well, hello there," she purred.

I almost rolled my eyes. Seriously, hadn't any of these people seen a vampire B-movie? I noticed they tended to use phrases that sounded like bad acting, but were sincere. It was both funny and irritating.

"Excuse me," I said politely. "I'm here with Lex, Donna, and Conner."

She leaned closer, putting her nose almost against my shoulder, and inhaled. It creeped me out a little, but I stood still. When she was done, she straightened, regret on her face.

"Damn, there goes my afternoon snack," she muttered. "If Lex is going to bring a treat he doesn't want to share, he should mark it somehow."

My first instinct was to scowl at her and ask her who the fuck she thought she was. I managed to keep that under control. Just. Instead, I murmured an almost indecipherable apology and skirted around her. I walked straight over to Lex. From the expression on his face, he had heard everything. He looked pained, as though he wanted to laugh but knew that I would be angrier if he did.

When I reached him, I looked at Donna but stomped hard on Lex's toe. While he cursed, I moved over to my girlfriend. She looked pale and worried. As soon as I was within arm's reach, she yanked me against her, hugging me so tight my back popped.

"Oh God, I'm sorry, Ivie," she said, releasing me.

"It's okay. I needed to have my back adjusted after that five hour ride in the car." I didn't mention the forty-five minute ride Lex had given me on the cabin floor, which had a lot to do with the stiffness in my muscles as well.

I faced Conner. "Do you have any new information?" I asked.

He had called and kept Lex and I updated as we drove in, but I hoped perhaps they had news since the last call an hour ago.

Conner shook his head.

"Do you know what they want?" I asked.

I watched as Conner's face shut down. Lex's expression was blank and Donna just looked worried as hell.

"Okay, will someone please share?" I asked.

Lex leaned down and put his mouth directly to my ear, speaking almost soundlessly. "We can't discuss it here. Too many eyes and ears."

I stared up at him. "Then let's go somewhere we damn well can."

Lex caught my hand in his and squeezed gently. "Later."

"But…"

He squeezed my hand again, looking at me as though he were trying to tell me something very important. "Later."

It suddenly occurred to me that The Faction was still recruiting new members and they might very well have spies in this very room, so I just tightened my grip on his hand and nodded.

Lex's eyes softened slightly.

"I need your attention, please."

Conner's announcement somehow boomed throughout the room without him raising his voice. It was a very cool trick. The dull roar that filled the ballroom became silent. When the last voice stopped speaking, Conner moved toward the center of the room, everyone circling around him.

"Thank you all for showing your support to the vampire nation," he continued. "I have called you here today because of a situation that has come to light the last few months. There is a group that is moving against the Vampire Council. They are not honorable and intend to use whatever means necessary to achieve their goals, including harming our loved ones." He looked around the room. "Those who are allied with the Council may also be targeted. You must take measures to protect your people."

I was only listening to Conner with half an ear because the woman who had stopped me earlier caught my attention. She was standing very still and appeared to be listening intently to every word Conner spoke. But something about her just seemed off. I realized that she didn't look stressed, tired, or even worried. In fact, she appeared smug to me.

I nudged Lex with my foot to get his attention then looked across the room at her. His gaze followed mine and his body tightened. I knew he saw what I did. I glanced at him out of the corner of my eye and saw him give Finn a look. Finn acknowledged whatever Lex was trying to tell him silently and began to casually move across the room toward the woman. Before he could get near her, she looked at me, winked, and freaking disappeared into thin air.

I knew Lex saw it as well because he touched Conner's back and leaned in to say something in his ear.

"I'm afraid that more information has just come in and must be acted upon now. If you have further questions, speak to Asher Leroux and he will answer them." Conner raised a hand. "Calder Atwood, could I speak to you for a moment?"

The room began to clear out, but Calder remained. As soon as everyone was gone, Conner and Lex began speaking at once.

"Ivie, tell me exactly what happened," Conner demanded.

Lex wrapped an arm around my shoulders. "How did you know?" he asked.

Donna blinked. "Know what? What did I miss?"

I looked at them all. "That woman," I began.

"Pat," Lex interrupted.

I blinked at him. "What?"

"Her name is Pat."

Donna raised an eyebrow. "Really?" she said incredulously. "The Vampire Pat just doesn't sound menacing. You guys need to work on your name choices because you kind of suck at it."

Conner looked like he wanted to tell her to shut up. Instead he sucked in a deep breath and pinched the bridge of his nose. "Pat is short for Cleopatra. You know, *the* Cleopatra."

My eyes widened.

"Can vampires get headaches?" I clamped my mouth shut as all eyes came to me. Shit, I hadn't meant to say that.

"I never had a headache after I was turned until six months ago," Conner said dryly.

"Hey!" Donna exclaimed.

"Excuse me, people," Calder drawled, "but didn't anyone notice this Pat bitch disappearing into thin air during this little meeting?"

I nodded, grateful to be off the subject of vampire headaches and domestic spats.

"How did you know something was wrong?" Lex asked again.

I shrugged. "I'm not sure. Everyone else was listening and at least looked concerned. She just seemed….off. I'm not sure why, except for that smug little smirk she was doing such a horrible job of hiding."

Conner looked at me with disbelief. "That's it? That's why you had Lex stop the meeting?"

I threw my hands in the air. "Well, when Finn started heading toward her, she looked straight at me, winked, and then *poof* she was gone! That doesn't exactly make her look innocent."

Lex spoke up then. "Finn was going to attempt to read her. I think Pat knew what was about to happen and made sure we couldn't glean any information from her."

Calder shifted from foot to foot, looking every inch the aggressive wolf he truly was. With his golden skin and hair and beautiful green-gold eyes, my other single girlfriends would be all over him in a hot minute. I kind of hoped he helped rescue them because they would at least get some great eye candy out of this entire hellish situation.

When I realized the insane tangent my thoughts had gone on, I mentally shook myself. I wasn't sure what was wrong with me, but this wasn't the time to be thinking about my remaining three single friends tackling the sexy werewolf and making him their sex slave. Even if it was funny.

Before the conversation continued, Conner's cell rang. He removed it from his pocket, glanced at the screen then froze.

"It's Pat," he said. He slid his finger across the screen and put the phone to his ear. "Hello?"

He listened for a moment, then held the phone out to Lex. "They want to speak to you."

Lex took the phone. "Lex," he clipped.

As he listened to the caller, his eyes grew colder, then began to glow. The color of his irises became clearer and more brilliant until I could no longer meet his gaze. Whatever this Pat was saying, it was pissing him off in a big way.

"Understood," he said abruptly before taking the phone and throwing it across the room in a blur of motion.

I took a step back, unsure what Lex might do next. Everyone else did as well. We watched as he stared at the ground, clenching and unclenching his fists.

"What did they want?" Conner asked softly.

Lex's head whipped up and round, his body strung tight.

"Your head, as well as the heads of three other Council members, by sunrise the day after tomorrow."

"Goddammit," Conner swore.

My wide eyes turned to Donna. I had a bad feeling that things just became extremely dangerous for our three friends. Aside from the three vampires in the room and me, no one else would really give a damn what happened to them because they were human.

At the sound of someone clearing their throat, all five of us whirled around to see a tall, curvaceous woman dressed in all black leaning against the wall. None of the supernatural beings in the room had heard or felt her enter. That alone made me worry.

"Hello, Conner," she said. She nodded to Lex. "Alexander."

Both vampires nodded in return. Though it seemed pretty clear that they weren't pleased with her arrival, they did seem to have a grudging respect for her.

"Belinda," Conner responded. "What can I do for the head of the Coven?"

I turned wide eyes to Donna. Holy shit, she was a witch. From what Conner just said, it sounded like she was *the witch*, as in top bitch.

She straightened from her casual position and sauntered toward us. "Well, you could start by explaining why one of our own has been taken, yet you did not bother to call us into your little meeting this afternoon," she said with a deceptively friendly tone.

"What?" Disbelief filled Conner's tone. "I have no idea what you're talking about."

Belinda seemed surprised. "Surely you knew you'd had a witch in your home recently."

Conner shrugged. "No, I didn't."

She tisked him as she shook her head. "That Kerry has become one hell of a powerful witch."

Donna went rigid. "You mean Kerry Gayle?" she asked.

Belinda turned her eyes to my friend and smiled a cat's smile. "Yes, my dear."

I felt a smile tug at the corners of my own mouth. Everyone else in the room looked at me as though I had lost my mind.

"Why on earth are you smiling, you crazy whore?" Donna asked.

My grin grew wider as I looked at her, then Belinda. "Because that little piece of news means that the girls aren't completely defenseless while they are being held captive by those assholes. We may actually be able to get them out of there in one piece."

The witch met my eyes and studied me closely for a moment. "You're absolutely right, Ivie Lang. With the help of the Coven, Kerry and the other women will be safe."

I only hoped that we tore those fucking, kidnapping vampires a new asshole while we were at it because they obviously needed to be taught a lesson.

Chapter Twenty-One

"FOR THE LAST TIME, Ivie, you are not going with us," Lex and Donna said in unison.

I scowled at the pair of them. "I won't go inside, I'll stay hidden in the vehicle or down the street, but I am going."

"I forbid it," Lex stated, crossing his arms over his chest.

I copied his movement. "And you're not the boss of me." Great, now I sounded like a petulant child. I glared at Lex and said, "Either you can take me with you, or I will follow you. Your choice how that goes."

Lex began to stalk toward me, all six-foot plus of pissed off alpha male. "Well, then. Perhaps I should chain you to the bed or lock you in Conner's basement. Both sound appealing at the moment."

I completely ignored how hot he was when he was angry, though it was extremely difficult. I focused on him, trying to find that connection. When it locked into place, I raised my hand. "Stop."

Amazingly enough, he did. Lex stared at me in shock. "How did you…"

Donna realized something was up and began to move toward us. I didn't know if it would work, but I had to try. I reached out to her, the thread between us snapping taut much more easily than it had with Lex.

"Go sit," I said, using my other hand to point to the chair a couple of feet from her.

Looking both surprised and annoyed, Donna turned and walked to the chair. She began to fight as her body lowered, slowing her progress but unable to stop it. It was then that they both began to fight me in earnest and my concentration wavered. It was the first time I tried something like this and I was shocked at how well it worked.

Ever since Lex said I could call him, it had been in the back of my mind that perhaps my abilities extended beyond conversations with vampires, but to actual control. Which sounded awesome, because I decided it might be fun to get a little payback against the assholes who jerked me around and messed with my brain. It also occurred to me that maybe I could use the skill to keep vampires from ever controlling me again. I hadn't mentioned it to anyone for fear that the wrong person would discover my ability and decide the vampire population was better off with me dead.

Finally, I couldn't contain their struggles any longer and I released my hold on Donna and Lex. Donna popped out of the chair like a jack-in-the-box.

"Wow, how the fuck did you do that? If I wasn't so freaked out and pissed off at you right now, I'd be impressed," she said.

Lex merely stood a couple of feet from me, staring at me with a blank expression on his face.

Donna continued, "If those people that the vampires killed all those years ago had your abilities, I can see why they might want them dead." As soon as she realized what she'd said, a look of horror crossed her face. It was almost comical, except I had been concerned about the same thing. "Oh God, we have to keep this a secret," she said frantically. "I don't know how the Council would react to this. It could be very, very bad."

Lex nodded in agreement. "Yes, it could." He never took his eyes from me. "Ivie, may I have a word with you in private, please?"

Oh shit. Now it looked like I was about to be reprimanded. I wanted to squirm both with fear and excitement. I never knew how Lex might react when he was angry. He might yell and walk away to calm down, or he might spank me and fuck out his anger.

I followed him out of the den and down the hall to the half bath. I paused when he held the door of the bathroom open and gestured for me to go first. He was a large man and it would be a tight fit. As soon as I was through the door, he crammed himself in next to me and shut and locked the door. Before I could blink, he had my hair wrapped around his fist and was pressing me belly-first into the wall.

I felt his lips touch my ear as he leaned into me, flattening me against the unforgiving surface.

"Do you know what you could have done?" Lex hissed.

I was wrong. He was beyond angry. I didn't speak, only shook my head.

His hips pressed into mine and I could feel him getting hard against my lower back. As he ground into me, he spoke, "If anyone other than Donna, Conner, Finn, or myself had seen you pull that little stunt, you would have been killed. Either in that instant or a convenient 'accident' would have occurred in a few weeks or months time. Though the Council will not admit to it, I know for a fact that several of them have had people such as yourself killed. There are a few that had important ties, families, or other powers that were forcibly turned, but it is rare." His voice was so deep it was practically an inaudible growl.

"Forcibly turned?" My voice wavered.

"Yes. Why don't you ask Finn what he thinks about it? He was like you. Able to control vampires while he was human. When they turned him, not only could he control them, he could also read their minds with ease. He's one of the most powerful of us and it's not because of his age. Though he killed his maker and those who plotted to use him, it still did not undo what was done."

Well, I had definitely almost screwed the pooch. "I understand," I said quietly.

Lex's grip on my hair loosened slightly. "I know you do. I merely wanted to impress upon you the importance of keeping this between the five of us. No one else can know."

"Okay."

Just as quickly as he pressed me to the wall, Lex yanked me back, turning me so that I faced him. I gasped as his hands grasped my waist and he lifted me to sit on the vanity by the sink.

"And you will not go with us tonight when we meet to do the exchange with The Faction. It is too dangerous and they have to know I won't deliver what they want. We are certain this is an elaborate trap."

I shook my head stubbornly. "I'm going."

Lex growled, pressing his erection right against my clit. "You will do as I say."

"No!"

His eyes flared and my body jerked as he tore away the center of my pants and my underwear. "You will stay here."

I met his eyes, refusing to back down on this. "I'm going. If you try to make me stay here, I will stop you and I will go without you."

His eyes brightened until they were difficult to meet, the chocolate brown lightening to brilliant topaz. I fought back a moan as his fingers slid across my clit and down, pressing deep inside me. I knew it was completely twisted but I was equally pissed off and turned on. I lifted my hips in time with the strokes of his hand. Then his fingers were gone.

Lex's stare never left mine and he put his palm to his mouth and licked from the base of his thumb to the tips of the fingers that had been inside me. It was fucking hot. When I felt the head of his dick prodding my pussy, I realized he was using the combination of his saliva and my own wetness to ease his way.

My eyes never left his as he pushed into me, sliding home with a single thrust. I took every inch, reveling in the slight burn as my body opened to his invasion. Then he grabbed my hips and began to move, hard and fast. I knew I would be bruised later, but that ramped up my arousal further.

"I'm going to fuck you so raw you won't be able to follow us," he said, sounding no less pissed off than he had earlier.

For the first time, I didn't give way to his demands. Instead, I demanded. I grabbed the short strands of hair at the nape of his neck and yanked his head back.

"I'm coming with you and I don't care what you say. It's happening."

Lex groaned, fucking me harder and causing the vanity to shake beneath me. I felt the muscles in my lower body tightening and knew that I wouldn't last much longer.

"Please, Lex."

His eyes were hot and piercing when he finally caved. "Fine, but you stay in the car."

"Okay," I said breathlessly.

The relentless pounding of his pubic bone against my clit finally threw me into a climax so intense that I lunged forward and sank my teeth into the upper part of his pectoral. When I broke the skin and tasted blood, Lex shouted and I knew he was coming.

As the frantic movement of his hips slowed and finally stopped, I leaned back against the mirror behind me, licking my lips. His blood tasted sweet and only slightly coppery, nothing like the flavor of my own.

"I'm sorry," I murmured.

His hands smoothed down my sides and hips over my pants and I realized that he had ripped the front of the jeans I was still wearing. I wanted to shake my head and laugh, but I was too relaxed.

"For what?" he asked.

"I didn't mean to bite you so hard."

Lex threw his head back and laughed. I did smile then because I always loved seeing him laugh. Still chuckling, he leaned forward and kissed me lightly on the lips, the first kiss he'd given me since he dragged me into the bathroom.

"You can bite me like that any time you like. Biting is foreplay for vampires. Especially if it draws blood. It adds to the experience."

I tilted my head to the side and looked at him. "You didn't bite me."

"I didn't want to risk weakening you in case I couldn't convince you not to come tonight."

I nodded. That was a good plan.

"Actually, if you're insisting on being there tonight, you should probably drink a little more of my blood."

I gaped at him. "What?"

Lex's face grew serious. "It will bolster your physical strength, help you heal, and will keep other vampires from controlling you with their minds. Well, mostly. A very strong vampire would be able to persuade you anyway, but there are very few who would manage it. My blood may also boost your natural powers and make you stronger. If something goes wrong, you would be able to get away."

Any other time he might have mentioned this, I would have said no immediately, but tonight was important. My life and the lives of people I loved would be at risk. I couldn't afford to be weak.

"I'll do it," I said before I could think too deeply about it.

Lex stared at me in surprise. "You will?"

I nodded. "Yes. I want to be as prepared as possible. You never know, you might need me to save your ass," I quipped.

Lex cupped my shoulders with his hands. "This is serious, Ivie."

I frowned at him. "I know it is, Lex."

He shook his head. "You don't understand. If you take my blood, you will be tied to me in the eyes of vampire law. When a vampire shares his or her blood with a human, it is meant to be a gesture of love or honor. It means we hold that person in the highest regard. It also means that our lives are connected from now on. You would not be able to escape from me then, even if you never allowed me to Claim you and turn you."

I blinked up at him, realizing exactly what he was offering me. "So this is like the vampire equivalent of going steady?" I asked.

Lex rolled his eyes. "It's a bit more complex than that, but, yes, it's a big deal."

"Do you love me?" I asked.

Lex frowned at me. "Yes. You know I do."

"Well, I love you, too. So, I think I can handle being tied to you."

He looked down at the wound on his chest. I wasn't surprised to see that the bite marks had healed almost completely. All that was left was a bright pink imprint of my teeth.

"I will bite my wrist. You will only need to draw a couple of mouthfuls but the wound will close quickly, so do not hesitate."

I nodded and watched as he lifted his wrist to his mouth. He bit down and then quickly put his arm to my mouth. I put my lips around the wound and sucked. I pulled twice before I swallowed, amazed at the taste of his blood. I would have thought that I would find this act repugnant, but it felt incredibly intimate and sexy.

I wasn't the only one who thought so. Lex was still inside me. As I began to suckle the wound on his wrist, his cock hardened and he began to move. I managed to get one more small mouthful of blood before the wound closed, but, by then, he was fully erect. He was gentle this time, though his hips were moving quickly.

Lex shoved my shirt above my breasts and yanked down the cups on my bra with one hand. His other hand snaked to the small of my back, forcing me to arch, and his lips closed around my nipple, sucking hard. The small flame of arousal exploded into an inferno within me. I wrapped my legs around his hips as he continued to nip and suckle my breasts. My hands buried themselves in his hair and I tugged his face toward mine.

He kissed me then, our tongues tangling. The hand that held my breast moved down my torso until his thumb rested on my clit. Lex began to rub firmly. Within minutes, I was on the edge again. My back arched as the orgasm washed over me. Lex followed me a few moments later.

After we both caught our breath, I cleaned up with a cloth Lex found in a drawer and he helped me climb off the counter. I glanced down at my destroyed pants then looked back up at him.

"Um, Lex, how am I going to get out of here without showing my goods to everyone in the house?"

When he saw the state of my pants, he chuckled. "Maybe you can command all the vampires to close their eyes," he quipped.

I narrowed my eyes at him. "How about I command you to go get me some damn pants since you're the reason my current pair is ruined?"

He smirked at me. "I think I can manage that."

I watched him leave, the smile disappearing from my face as the door shut behind him. Though I didn't tell him, I was terrified of what the evening might bring. I just hoped that we all made it out alive.

Chapter Twenty-Two

I SAT ALONE in the third row of the SUV. Donna, Conner, and Finn were all in the front, completely silent. Lex was in the sedan in front of us, a huge duffel bag in the back that contained several mannequin heads. I asked why he bothered with the ruse and he said that it would appear in the beginning as though he complied with their demands, perhaps giving the rest of the vampires, weres, and witches time to get into position.

We were on our way to the meet with representatives from The Faction. Belinda the Good Witch, which is how I thought of her, had managed to contact Kerry and we knew that the girls were being held in the same location as the meet. Whether The Faction intended to honor their promise to Lex or not, we were headed right for them.

I was worried about him. He would be alone with them for a bit before the horde descended upon the building. I knew he had been a general and a warrior his entire existence, but that didn't mean he was completely immortal. I knew from all the questions I asked Donna after she was turned that vampires were not as hard to kill as the lore suggested.

I didn't understand the entire plan, though I did know that Lex would go in and give the signal to strike. Calder's pack and Belinda's coven were there for back up, as were the four vampires

Lex said he could trust; Donna, Conner, Finn, and Asher, who I had only met once.

With the information Kerry provided to Belinda, we knew there were between five and ten vampires in the building at any given time. She had also given Belinda information that had made the witch's face look pale and pinched. Apparently, The Faction had a warlock on their payroll. According to Belinda, this took the operation up from a low danger level to on par with dismantling an armed nuclear device. Warlocks were witches that had gone bad and they liked to leave nasty little booby traps to protect themselves. We were going to have to be very, very careful.

Conner began to slow the SUV and I realized we had reached the edge of the perimeter that Belinda had set based on the magical survey her coven had done of the grounds surrounding the building. I watched as the sedan that Lex drove disappeared around a bend in the road, my heart sinking. It was beginning.

Conner had instructed Donna and I to stay in the car until he signaled for us. We fully intended to follow those commands as long as the boys didn't run into any trouble.

If they did step into a pile of shit, Donna had told Conner, "All bets are off, Fangboy."

The vampire knew Donna well enough not to argue, though he did look as though he wanted to throttle her.

Conner pulled the SUV over onto the shoulder. Finn opened the passenger door and climbed out.

"I'm off to help the witches," he said. "I think they'll need a bit more power than they have, and nothing is quite as powerful as vampire blood when added to a spell."

I had no idea what he meant, but nodded to him anyway. "Be careful, Finn."

He winked at me, shut the door, and disappeared into the trees along the side of the road. He moved so quickly all I saw was a blur. I began to gnaw on my thumbnail, eyes on the place where he had vanished.

"Don't worry, Ivie. Finn has magic in his blood. He was a caster of spells long before he became a vampire. He will be fine."

My eyes moved to the rearview mirror, meeting the bright blue of Conner's gaze and I nodded.

"It's been three minutes. Any word from Lex?" Donna asked.

Conner shook his head. "I haven't received the signal yet."

I had no idea how Lex intended to signal Conner. I'd asked, but he'd merely said, "It's complicated."

"We go in if we haven't heard from him after seven minutes, right?" she asked, worry plain in her voice.

I didn't say anything, but seven minutes just seemed like an arbitrary number to me. Why not five or ten?

"Yes, Donna." Conner's voice was tight with stress.

I moved my gaze to the back of Donna's neck until she turned and looked at me. I gave a tiny shake of my head, warning her to be patient and not pester Conner. He needed to be focused. She sighed but didn't say anything else.

The minutes ticked by so slowly that I thought I was going insane. At the six minute mark, there was still no word from Lex. My heart was beating fast and hard in my chest. This couldn't be good.

Suddenly, blue fire exploded about thirty feet to our right, so bright that it was clearly visible through the trees. Conner shifted the SUV into drive.

"I think that is our fucking cue." He peeled out and sped down the road, going the same direction as Lex had. "Remember, stay in the goddamn car until I call for you. I'm leaving the vehicle in the trees near the building. Do not leave it or I will blister both your asses."

Donna made an annoyed sound, but I just squeaked. His threat to blister my ass didn't sound nearly as fun as when Lex did it.

"Goddamn, fucking mistake to bring you two along," I heard him mutter under his breath.

"It was your only choice and you know it. If you hadn't brought us with you, we would have followed anyway," Donna retorted.

Conner didn't respond because he was steering the car off the road, barely slowing down. He shot between two trees, mowing down smaller brush and saplings until the SUV was hidden from the road. Through the branches of the tree to our left, I saw a building with the sedan Lex had driven parked in front of it, all four doors and the trunk open, and not a single vampire in sight. This was not good.

Conner turned and pinned us both with a harsh blue stare. "Stay down, be careful, and do not hesitate to kill if necessary. If you hesitate, you will die."

With those ominous words, he leapt from the car and shut the door behind him. He rapped on the window next to Donna.

"Lock the doors."

She nodded and reached over the driver's seat to hit the automatic lock button. Conner didn't move, merely pointed downward with his index finger. I understood he was being perfectly serious about us staying down. I climbed on to the floorboard and turned so I could see between the seats in front of me where the arm rest had been lowered.

Donna pressed her hand to the glass of the window. "I love you, Conner. Be careful."

He winked at her as Finn had winked at me and left so quickly that I had no idea which direction he was headed. Donna did the same thing I had done, crouching on the floorboard but facing me so we could see each other over the armrest.

Somewhere nearby another explosion ripped through the trees, making the SUV shake and casting an eerie blue light inside the vehicle. I pulled my knees into my chest and wrapped my arms tightly around them. Then the howling began and I knew the werewolves had arrived.

A few moments later I heard the screams of a woman quickly cut off. My wide eyes met Donna's and she reached through the opening between the seats. I took her hand in mine and squeezed.

"It will be okay, Ivie," she reassured me.

I didn't respond. I hoped she was right, but I was also worried that she was wrong. More explosions and cries of pain drifted through the trees around us, along with howls and yips from the wolves. Some close, some further away. I wasn't sure how much time had passed, just that it felt like an eternity.

Finally everything around us fell silent. Not even the birds were chirping. Yet a heavy layer of energy seemed to cover everything. It was oppressive. Strangely, I felt as though it were waiting to lash out and injure anyone that might be stupid enough to remain in the woods.

As the quiet dragged on, Donna looked to me. "This isn't good," she muttered.

"What?"

"Conner has cut himself off from me. He did it a few moments ago."

"I don't understand," I said.

"After he turned me, I developed a telepathic link with Conner. Now, he's shut it down on his end. That can only mean one thing."

My eyes widened as I understood what she was implying.

"He's either severely injured or he thinks he's dying." She raised her head and peeked out the window behind her, toward the building. "I can't sit here, just a few hundred feet away, and do nothing while he dies."

I nodded. She was right. If Conner was in trouble, so was Lex. I couldn't sit by and let him die.

"So, what do we do?" I asked.

She opened her mouth and I knew she was going to tell me to stay in the car. I lifted a hand to her.

Using the connection between us, I commanded, "Do not tell me to stay in the car."

The look on her face would have been hilarious if the situation hadn't been so dire. She wanted so badly to say those words, but I was keeping her from doing it. After a few seconds, I released my hold over her.

"So what's the plan?" I prompted.

She grimaced at me. "I don't have a plan exactly, except to go in and get our men and our friends and kill any bastards who get in the way."

I nodded. "Sounds simple enough."

She looked out the windows one more time, staying low. Then I watched as she crawled into the seat in front of me and lifted the mat off the floorboard where she had been sitting. There was a little trapdoor beneath it. My eyes bugged out of my head as she opened it to reveal three handguns.

"Do you know how to use one of these?" she asked.

I shook my head. Except for the time I'd almost shot Conner, I'd never held a gun in my life, much less fired one. I watched as she pulled it out, fiddled with it for a second until a clip popped out. She checked the clip, I assumed to see if it was full, before she put them back in. She pulled back the slide and revealed the bullet in the chamber as well.

Then she popped the clip back into the gun and repeated the process with the other weapon. She reached back into the hiding spot and pulled out two more clips, which she checked over.

"Since you can't shoot, you need to stay right on my tail. No deviating from my path, no running off," she stated calmly. "I'm faster and stronger than you, so I can block an attack long enough for you to do your mind control thing and then I'll shoot whoever needs to be shot."

"What if we run into the warlock?" I asked.

Donna looked at me. "I don't know, but I guess I'll try to shoot the bastard."

I knew it was the best plan we could come up with considering we were out of time if we wanted to help Lex and Conner.

"Okay."

She stuck her head up again, looking all around the SUV. I assumed the coast was clear because she said, "Crawl through but try to stay low."

I gave her a look. "Why don't you lower one side of the seats?" I asked. No use trying to wriggle over the top and draw attention to ourselves when I could just creep over the flattened seat.

She rolled her eyes. "Dammit, I'm glad you thought of that." Then she reached over and lowered the passenger side seat.

I moved over the seat and on to the floor board in front of her. Donna reached forward and grabbed the car keys out of the ignition, shoving them into her pocket.

"We're going to get out of the car on the driver's side, at the same time," she said. "But, first, I'm going to look on top of the car and beneath it just in case something nasty is waiting for us."

I nodded, glad she thought to check. I watched, holding my breath, as she opened the door just enough to stick her head out and look up. Then she peeked quickly beneath the car. She pulled the door closed without latching it shut.

"We're all clear. We're going to move quickly and as quietly as possible. There's nothing to hide behind in the fifty feet between the trees and the building, so you have to move as fast as possible."

I nodded.

"Ready?"

I nodded again, scared out of my mind that we were taking too much time, and that Conner and Lex would be dead by the time we got inside.

Faster than I could see, Donna was out of the car, pulling me right along behind her. She quickly opened the driver's door, locked the car, and shut both doors almost silently. I just barely heard the latches catch, but she winced as though they were a gunshot.

"Move, move, move," she urged, running so fast I could barely keep up. "Any supernatural being would have heard that."

I knew she was right and my heart turned to stone in my chest when I realized exactly how much danger we were in. We reached the edge of the building. Donna held a gun in one hand and my arm in another. She wasn't taking any chances that we would be separated. She peeked around the corner and the coast must have been clear because she made a beeline for the front door.

A few seconds later, we were inside. I released the breath I had been holding when my vision began to turn black around the edges. I sucked in a breath as quietly as possible, but Donna gave me a look that said even that was too loud.

We crept down the hall, my front practically against her back. The building was oddly silent. My heart was pounding so hard, I was sure that any vampire in the building could hear it. We drew closer to a door at the end of the short hallway and Donna gestured for me to stop. There were faint noises coming from the other side.

She brought my hand to her belt at the back of her jeans and gave me a look that said to hold on tight. Then used her now free hand to slowly and silently turn the door knob. The door made no sound as it swung open. The room in front of us was pitch black.

Donna kept her gun tucked close to her front as she peeked around the door frame. I knew her night vision was much better than mine, but my skin still crawled when she nodded to me and began to move into the room. I followed her step for step, praying that the room was empty of bad creatures.

The noises I heard before were getting louder and the muscles in my neck began to lock up. I just knew that something was behind me, but every time I glanced back, all I saw was the rectangle of light coming in from the open door behind us.

Finally, Donna stopped and she must have been opening another door, because a dim light began to fill the room. I barely suppressed a gasp when I saw that the floor around us was strewn with bodies. There were at least five men and women scattered around the room, but I couldn't tell exactly how many because some were missing body parts, such as legs, arms, and even heads.

I wanted to puke at the sight of so much blood, but I was frozen in shock and fear. Only the tap of Donna's hand on my arm brought me back to the present. She was staring at me with concern in her eyes, but I swallowed back the sickness that wanted to spill into my throat and nodded at her, telling her to go on.

She repeated the process of peeking out the door and I realized that the noises I had been hearing were the thuds of fists on flesh and grunts of pain. When Donna turned to look at me, she lifted five fingers and mouthed the words, bad guys. I nodded. She then mouthed Lex and Conner's names and gave me a thumbs up.

I blew out a silent sigh of relief. Even if they were hurt, at least Lex and Conner were still fighting. She grinned at me and held up three fingers. Setting a slow beat with her fist, she began a silent countdown as her fist dropped, she tucked another finger in. When all three fingers were down, she began to move out into the room.

I tried not to scream when I saw that Lex was fighting off two other vampires that carried freaking swords. He only had a huge iron rod that he picked up from somewhere and his shirt was in tatters, his torso covered in cuts and blood. Conner was taking on three men, a fourth lying headless on the floor. In Conner's hands was an enormous battle axe. I assumed he took it off the dead vampire because I knew damn well he hadn't gone in carrying one.

Conner must have seen us out of the corner of his eye because his head snapped around, breaking his focus on the fight. One of his opponents slashed his thigh with a sword, causing him to cry out and go down on one knee.

I flinched at the loud boom of the gun as Donna raised it and fired at the vampire who had cut her man. The bullet caught him in the shoulder, but all it seemed to do was piss him off. He started toward us, a blur of motion. The gun went off so many times I lost count, until it was empty. The vamp was still coming.

I was frozen in shock, unable to focus enough to try and make the mental connection needed to stop him, when I saw the battle axe swing through the air and sever the approaching vampire's head.

I gave a short scream as blood sprayed everywhere and the bad guy's body flopped lifelessly to the floor. Without sparing me a glance, Donna dropped the spent clip and reloaded the gun. Conner had turned away from us to face the other two men.

I looked over at Lex and almost cried out again when I saw that he was distracted by our arrival as well. Somehow he managed to take out one of the vampires he had been fighting when we entered, but his other opponent had used the opportunity to pierce him through the gut with his sword. I watched in horror as the vamp yanked the sword out of Lex's stomach, causing a rush of blood to leave my man's body.

The shock that froze me earlier disappeared and rage filled me. Without thinking twice, I reached out to that thread that I felt connecting me to all the vampires in the room, determining who was who. Within a split second I grasped three threads with my mind.

"STOP!" I shrieked.

Amazingly, all three of the remaining bad guys froze in place, not even batting an eyelash or making a sound. Lex, Conner, and Donna were all staring at me in shock. I pointed to the two Conner had been fighting.

"Kill him," I commanded. I was speaking to both of them.

Woodenly, they turned to one another and swung their swords simultaneously. I watched with cold satisfaction as their heads separated from their bodies and they fell to the floor. Then I turned to the vampire who had been ready to kill Lex.

"Ivie, wait," Conner said. "We need him alive. He may have information we need."

I barely stopped myself from giving the vampire the order to disembowel himself. I wanted to see him suffer for what he had just done to Lex.

"I'll take the bastard," a voice said.

I looked around and didn't see anything. Suddenly Finn appeared out of thin air, causing Donna and I both to jump. He was grinning at me.

"Good job, Ivie. I couldn't have done better myself if I had arrived in time."

I nodded to him, the adrenaline hitting me out of nowhere, causing my hands to shake as I pushed my hair off my face.

Finn walked to the other vampire and placed a hand against his forehead while I forced the bad guy to remain still. He fought me hard, but the rage and adrenaline coursing through my body made me strong. I wasn't sure what Finn was doing to the vampire, but his eyes rolled back in his head and he trembled as though he was having a stroke. All the while, Finn kept his palm on the vampire's forehead, eyes closed.

A few moments later, he opened his eyes and the vampire went limp, falling to the floor.

"I know where the women are and everything this sad sack of shit knows about The Faction. You can do what you wish with him."

Before I could react to Finn's words, Lex grabbed the sword that had fallen to the floor and cleaved the vampire's head from his body. That done, he tossed the sword to the side, looking every inch the battle-hardened warrior he'd been while human.

"Donna, I do believe you and I need to discuss what the words *wait in the car* mean?" Conner said through clenched teeth.

I watched in horror and awe as my friend waved a hand at her pissed off vampire mate. "Pipe down, Fangboy. We saved your ass, didn't we?"

"It was under control," Conner said softly.

I chanced a look at Lex. Whether I saved his ass or not, I knew from that one look that I probably wouldn't sit comfortably for at least a week. Not for the first time, I wondered why I had to fall in love with a fucking kinky vampire.

Chapter Twenty-Three

THOUGH LEX LOOKED as though he were ready to strangle me, I walked slowly over to him, stepping around headless bodies and one head.

As I got closer, I said softly, "I'm sorry I made you angry, but I'm glad you're going to be okay."

When I was within reach, he grabbed me by my shoulders and jerked me into a hard embrace.

His lips brushed my hair in a light kiss. "Don't ever scare me like that again," he whispered. "I thought I would lose you for sure."

I pressed my body closer to his, not caring that I was getting his blood all over my clothes. I was just relieved he was still standing.

"I can't promise that," I murmured, tilting my head back to meet his eyes. "Any time I think you're in danger, my first instinct will be to protect you. I love you."

Lex sighed, brushing my hair back from my face and kissing my forehead. "That is a pretty apology, little one, and it makes me happy to know how deeply you care for me, but it won't save you from punishment."

I scowled at him. "I don't give a damn about punishment. I just want you safe."

"And that's what I want for you," Lex said.

I continued to frown at him. "We'll discuss this later."

He nodded and released me. I turned to Finn. "Where are Ricki, Kerry, and Shannon?" I asked.

He was grinning at me. "They are in a small storage room at the back of the building. I think it's best if the two of you are the ones to open the door. I do believe your friend, Kerry, intends to fry any vampire, werewolf, or witch that dares to enter."

We followed Finn through the building. I tried not to look at the carnage that surrounded us. There were a great deal more than ten vampires in this building. And I was pretty sure most of them were the enemy. Anxiety tightened my chest when I thought about the number of vampires that might already be in The Faction. The thoughts I was having terrified me.

We approached a door and Finn stood to one side. "This is it," he said.

I stepped closer. "Kerry? Shannon? Ricki? It's me, Ivie."

At first there was silence, before I heard Kerry's voice. "Prove it."

"Well, I guess we could talk about Pete from college who begged to dip your toes in chocolate and suck...."

I never finished the sentence.

"Okay, I know it's you," Kerry yelled.

I grinned as Donna giggled. "I'm going to open the door now. Donna is with me and so is Conner. Lex and Finn are here also. Please don't zap any of us, okay?"

"Okay," she agreed.

I stepped back and Conner grasped one of the three padlocks on the door, breaking them off one at a time. When he was done, Donna and I opened the door slowly.

Kerry, Ricki, and Shannon were all standing in the farthest corner of the small room, backs to the wall.

"About time you got here," Ricki quipped. "And why didn't anyone tell me about the fucking vampires?"

I smiled and shook my head. "Well, what are you waiting for, an invitation? Get out here."

They all smiled and came out of the room, blinking in the harsh overhead lighting after being locked in the dark for two days. Donna and I moved forward, the five of us hugging each other tightly.

When I released the girls, I realized that Kerry hadn't met Lex yet. She had been absent at Conner and Donna's engagement party. Probably because she was a witch and she knew that the place would be full of vampires. I realized that the only time she came around was when it was just Conner and Donna alone. Any other vampires and she disappeared.

"Kerry, this is Lex Dimitriades. We're sort of together now," I said, lifting a hand toward my vampire.

She nodded to him. "Hi, Sexy Lexy. Thanks for saving our asses."

Conner chuckled and Lex merely smiled, seemingly unaffected by her silly nickname. Then I gestured to Finn.

"And this is Conner and Lex's friend, Finn."

When Kerry looked at him, her face paled. For a moment I thought she was going to faint. I glanced at Finn and saw that his expression was similarly dumbstruck.

"It's you," he said.

Kerry began to shake her head. "It can't be. It can't be." She turned to Donna and Conner. "Get me out of here please."

Donna wrapped an arm around her, shushing her and guiding her away. I looked back at Finn, and every line on his body screamed out his desire to go to her. Then he blinked and the look of intense yearning on his face disappeared.

Shannon and Ricki looked at me. "What was that about?" Shannon asked.

I shrugged because I honestly didn't know.

"We'll find out," Ricki muttered under her breath. Then, in her normal voice, "Well, I need a shower. Will someone please take me home so I can take off these disgusting clothes and burn them?"

Lex stepped forward. "I'll take you ladies home."

"Thanks, Sexy Lexy," Ricki said, jumping right on the silly nickname bandwagon that Kerry had begun.

To my surprise, Lex didn't even bat an eye. Instead, he looked to me. "You should go back with Donna and Conner. I'll meet you at their place after I take Ricki and Shannon to get some clothes and then drop them off somewhere safe."

I blinked, surprised at his blank expression and bland words. Then I nodded. I did not want to get into a fight in front of my girlfriends. They didn't know Lex all that well, and I wanted them to think highly of him since he would probably be in my life for a very long time.

We all exited the building together. I found Donna and Conner standing next to the SUV we had ridden in on the way to the meet. It felt like days had passed, when it had been little more than an hour and half. Kerry was standing next to a car I didn't recognize, talking with Belinda. When she saw Finn come out with us, she said something to the coven leader and they both rounded the car to climb in. Kerry waved to me and made a 'call me' gesture with her hand to her ear. I nodded.

I looked over at Finn as the car reversed and drove away, my heart aching for him when I saw the naked longing on his face. Somehow he and Kerry knew one another and he wanted her badly. I decided then and there to give her a week to settle, then I was going to put on my matchmaker hat and work on getting the two of them talking.

I hugged Ricki and Shannon good bye and told them I would talk to them the next day. I promised to explain everything to them both. Ricki seemed to be taking everything in stride, especially the hot vampires, but Shannon was upset about more than the kidnapping and I could see it clearly on her face. We were all strung out and exhausted. I waved as I climbed into the back of the SUV and rode home with Conner and Donna in silence.

When we arrived at the house, I hugged Donna and Conner in turn. "I love you both," I said softly, a little embarrassed at my show of emotion.

Conner merely kissed my cheek. "Me too, sweet Ivie."

Donna wrapped her arms around me one more time as well. "Thanks for being my best bitch," she said. Her face grew serious then. "I really love you too, Ivie. You and all the girls."

Tears filled my eyes, but I blinked them back. "Okay, well, I'm disgusting, so I'm going to take a shower and head to bed."

She smiled slightly, her own eyes slightly wet. "Me too. See you in the morning?" she asked.

"Sounds like a plan."

We parted ways and I headed upstairs to the guest room I had been sharing with Lex. As soon as the door shut behind me, I went into the bathroom and stripped off all my clothes. After I turned on the shower, I combed all the tangles out of my hair, which took a while because of its length and the curls.

Then I stepped into the shower and stood under the spray for a long time. Long enough for the enormity of everything that had happened that day to hit me. I cried then. Huge, heaving sobs that wracked my entire body.

The jag was short-lived as exhaustion took over. I carefully washed and conditioned my hair, then used my shower gel to wash away the remnants of dirt, blood, and the stink of fear. Once I was squeaky clean, I turned off the water and dried myself off.

I walked back into the bedroom, surprised it was still empty. I had been in the bathroom a long time. I was too tired to bother with clothes, so I merely dropped my towel by the bed and climbed under the blankets, switching off the lamp as I went. A few seconds later, I was asleep.

✧ ✧ ✧

A FEW HOURS LATER, I opened my eyes as a large, warm body settled behind mine. Lex's arms wrapped around me, pulling me tightly against his chest.

"Are you still angry with me?" I whispered.

He squeezed me lightly. "We'll talk in the morning."

I knew that meant yes, so I struggled until he allowed me to turn over and face him. A little bit of moonlight came through the blinds in the bedroom, outlining his profile and making his dark eyes gleam. Gently, I touched his cheek, slightly reassured when he turned his head to press his lips into my palm.

"Please don't be angry with me anymore," I pleaded.

Lex sighed. "You put yourself in danger, Ivie, after I specifically told you to stay in the SUV."

"Yes, I did. And I would do it again. Just like you would do whatever it took to protect me, I would do the same for you."

He shook me slightly. "It's not the same."

"Why? Because I'm not a vampire? Because I'm weaker?" I asked. Then I answered my own question. "I don't think so, Lex. I think I proved today that I am in no way weaker than you. Are my strengths different than yours, yes, but I survived. I would never rush into a situation like that without some sort of plan and definitely back up."

He scoffed. "Back up? Who was your back up?"

"Donna."

"Donna was almost killed today."

"So were you," I replied. "And so was Conner." This conversation was going nowhere. Lex was utterly convinced he was right and there would be no changing his mind tonight. "Obviously, you aren't willing to see my point, but I will say one more thing. With the upheaval taking place in your world right now, any one of us could die on any given day. We can be vigilant and we can be prepared, but it is still a possibility. Does that mean we should run away and hide? I don't know about you, but I think that means that they win. And I don't want those assholes to win. The only way evil can prevail is when good people do nothing, Lex. I refuse to do nothing."

Lex was silent for a long moment before he sighed, his arms relaxing slightly. His lips touched my forehead, then my mouth. "You're right, little one."

His assent shocked me. I thought it would take at least another 48 hours of me arguing with his stubborn ass before he could at least concede my point.

"What?" I asked incredulously.

"You're right."

"What?"

He growled, his arms tightening around me again. "You heard me the first two times."

I grinned in the dark. "Sorry, I just thought it would be a while before you said those words to me again, so I wanted to be sure I remembered this moment."

Lex chuckled. "Don't worry, I'll make you pay for it."

I tucked my head under his chin, pressing my ear to his pectoral. "I look forward to it." I closed my eyes, settling in to go back to sleep, happy knowing that it was over. For now. "I love you," I murmured.

"I love you too."

Feeling content, I drifted to sleep, wrapped around my very own Greek warrior.

Epilogue

KERRY STOOD ON the balcony of her hotel room, staring out across downtown Dallas. Despite the horrors she'd faced over the last few days, she couldn't sleep. Or maybe it was because of them.

The night air was cool against her skin and the light of the full moon fed her power. If she were at her home in the country, she would have gone out at midnight, sky clad, and drawn down the moon. After the stresses of being kidnapped by vampires, her power was severely depleted. Though rest and a few potions would help her gain her strength quickly.

The word vampires echoed through her brain, drawing her thoughts to one in particular. Until Ivie had introduced them, she had no idea what he truly was. Though she had never met him in person, Kerry saw him in her dreams night after night.

Sometimes they would be sitting together quietly, working in her herb garden or studying old texts about magic. Others they would be arguing passionately about something, anything. Then there were the times that made her shiver, and not because she was standing in the cool night air. Those times, he would strip her naked and do things to her body that made her moan. He would take her, sometimes gentle, sometimes rough, but always she could see his unique eyes glowing in the dark. Bright and shimmering, like amethysts.

The night breeze blew through her hair, carrying with it a voice.

You are mine, Kerry Gayle. You know it as well as I do. Come to me.

Her heart ached to do just that. From the books she had studied, Kerry knew what her dreams meant. The man with incredible eyes was her mate, the other half of her soul. He was also her enemy. Finn. A vampire. Blood drinker.

She closed her eyes, trying to block out the beautiful voice that beckoned her. Kerry knew, if she gave in, he would lead her to her death.

The End

Acknowledgments

First of all, I need to thank my awesome betas, Tania and Amber for reading the book and giving me such great feedback. You ladies have been a huge help!

Also, thank you to Donna for getting me in touch with Tania, organizing my blog tours, listening to my ragey rants, making sure I meet deadlines, and talking me out of quitting when I get to that point in every book where I think everything I write sucks. Muah!

A HUGE thank you to The Whorehouse. The original five, who inspired this series, are such a great group of ladies. I love you all to bits. So, thank you, Donna, Ivie, Kerry, Ricki, and Shannon for allowing me to use your likeness and several of the hilarious situations and conversations we've had in the last year. Now that our group has grown to include Trinity, Desiree, Joanne, Cheryl, Suzy, Laurel, Tara, Buffy, and Angie, I may have to develop some new characters!

Lastly, I need to thank all the bloggers and readers who keep promoting and buying my books. I love you all so hard! Smoochies!

About C.C.

A native Texan, C.C. grew up either reading or playing the piano. Years later, she's still not grown up and doing the same things. Since the voices in her head never shut up, C.C. decided to try and profit from their crazy stories and started writing books.

Now that she has a baby girl at home, C.C.'s non-writing time is usually spent cleaning up poopy diapers or feeding the poop machine. Sometimes she teaches piano, cooks, or spends time bugging her hubby and two beagles.

Contact C.C.

C.C. loves to hear from her readers!

Facebook: www.facebook.com/authorccwood

Twitter: @cc_wood

Website: www.ccwood.net

Titles by C.C. Wood

Novellas:

Girl Next Door Series:
Friends with Benefits
Frenemies
Drive Me Crazy
Girl Next Door – The Complete Series

Kiss Series:
A Kiss for Christmas
Kiss Me

Novels:

Seasons of Sorrow

Paranormal Romance:

Bitten Series
Bite Me
Once Bitten, Twice Shy

Made in the USA
Lexington, KY
20 March 2019